A deeply heartfelt story ... Clarke understands the peculiar magic that is addressing a serious topic without taking oneself seriously in the process, and wields wit and wordplay with enviable skill. Pratchett and Adams fans, take note.

— TYLER HAYES, AUTHOR OF THE IMAGINARY CORPSE

Wonderfully charming and beautifully weird…

— AMANDA, BOOKISH BREWS

Farcical theatre at its best ... full of wit and charm.

— JOHN DEREK, GOODREADS USER

Clarke has keen insight, and *Judgment Dave* holds up a mirror to our present moment ... a hilarious tale wrapped around a warm, uplifting core.

— J. SCOTT COATSWORTH, AUTHOR OF THE STARK DIVIDE

Fun sci-fi that deftly balances irreverent comedy and prescience

— DAVE WALSH, AUTHOR OF BROKEN ASCENSION

Read this if you love queer space romps that have something important to say – and can still make you laugh.

Joining the *Teapot* crew again is like snuggling in a fuzzy blanket. It's just so wholesome and lovely.

For everyone whose mind is reeling from, well, everything and who can't cope with another serious novel about serious people dealing with serious problems. Not right now.

FROZEN HECK

A NOT-REMOTELY-SCARY SCI-FI HORROR NOVEL

STARSHIP TEAPOT #4

SI CLARKE

AUTHOR'S NOTE

This book is written in British English. If you're used to reading American English, some of the spelling and punctuation may seem unusual. I promise, it's totally safe.

This story also features a number of Canadianisms. Sadly, I cannot promise these are safe. You may find yourself involuntarily wearing a touque and craving Timbits and a double-double. It can't be helped. Seek treatment immediately.

Lastly, this book contains an inordinate number of geek culture references. This as an homage to all things science fiction. There are countless references to all my favourites – *Star Trek*, *Red Dwarf*, *Firefly*, *The X-Files*, *Doctor Who*, *Battlestar Galactica*, *Hitchhiker's Guide to the Galaxy*, *Babylon 5*, *The Expanse*, etc. None of it should be read as derogatory or dismissive, nor would I ever suggest my work can take the place of anyone else's. Please support artists and authors. This is my love song to the entire genre.

Okay, you know how in TV shows you get that little one-minute segment at the start of each episode to catch you up? Books should do that too, I think. Just a handy little reminder since it may have been a while since you read the previous books. Or maybe you're like me and you've jumped right in at book four. No judgement.

Previously on *Starship Teapot*... [You may want to imagine Anthony Stewart Head's voice reading this to you.]

Lem, a perfectly ordinary aro-ace agender IT project manager, is kidnapped by aliens while camping with her German shepherd, Spock. While trying to figure out how to get home, they make some new friends: a talking horse-person, an unswearing robot, an overly anxious parrot, and a cloud of sentient glitter gas. Along the way, Lem discovers that the universe is far stranger than she'd ever imagined.

One of the things Lem learns is that Darmok and Jalad were right: communication requires a shared frame of reference. So Holly, Lem's universal translator and personal AI, suggests using figurative mode to facilitate easier discourse.

'This will include facts you already know but may have forgotten,' it explained. 'I will also incorporate extrapolative and fictional sources. Your extensive knowledge of science fiction will provide a useful base for figurative mode.'

Early on in her new life in space, Lem encounters an alien.

She raised her arms. Wait, his arms? Their arms? I shook my head. Not the time to wonder about alien pronouns. I decided to stick with she until someone told me otherwise.

Much later, Lem learns that alien sex and gender are … complicated. The binary most people are used to on Earth doesn't apply.

'Hang on,' I said. 'If pronouns don't align to sex or gender because most species don't think that way … does that mean BB, Aurora, and Henry aren't women?'

So there are two pronouns: *she* for all sentient beings and *it* for all non-sentient/inanimate objects. And as for names…

'Back in the early days of translators, programmers tried to transliterate names of people and places,' said Bexley. 'But it was all "unintelligible noise this" and "awkward silence that". No, in the end, they decided the best thing for it was for people to make their own names for everyone they encounter. Once you assign a name to someone, your AI will remember it.'

That's right: it's literally impossible to misgender or dead-name someone. Whatever you may call a person, the translator will convert it to their preferred name or pronoun.

After two kidnappings and three escapes, Lem and the gang meet up in the pub. And when it's finally time to go home, Lem and Spock decide that, actually, they're more at home in this weird and wonderful universe than they ever were on Earth.

Lem and her new friends buy the *Teapot* and form a transport company. One of their first jobs is working for the Galactic Union (basically the space version of the EU). Later they – together with Bexley's family – get caught up in a widely publicised court case about the fundamental rights of unicorns and pegasuses.

———

And now … the next episode.

Alone in the universe. All alone … and dreaming about chocolate brownies.

I gazed up at the midnight black of space beyond the glass dome. When we were in warp, the stars didn't do like they did on telly. They didn't, you know, *voom*. They just kind of blurred around the edges.

To be fair, I wasn't even alone. The others weren't actually gone – they'd just retired to their rooms. Both BB and Spock slept more than I did, so it was fairly normal for me to be awake when they weren't. Bexley, Henry, and Aurora all required less rest than I did, so it was unusual for me to be the only one awake. But it happened occasionally.

And I wasn't even alone in the room. Spock was curled up on the sofa with me – but she was sound asleep, so it didn't really count. I'd woken up at half three in the morning and had been unable to get back to sleep. Bexley talked in her sleep sometimes.

So I came up here to gaze at the stars.

Under the room's clear dome was my favourite spot to

stand and gaze at the universe. I loved seeing the stars in all their glory.

We'd been working for Megaboulder and the Accountants of Doom, the band that had won last year's Space Eurovision. Our job was ferrying the band between shows. I'd seen plenty of recordings of their shows – I'd even watched the band doing sound checks and they'd done a few jam sessions on the *Teapot*. But I'd still never seen them play live. Always somewhere else to be, something else to do. This time, we were going to make the time to see the show on Felspoon.

Megaboulder had given us front-row seats. The horta was terrifying to look at – just big piles of animate rocks. But she was genuinely one of the nicest people I'd ever met.

Taking care not to wake Spock, I got up and walked to the outer edge of Ten Backwards – our crew lounge and meeting space.

'Ow!' Less than a metre from the window, something jolted me. 'Bloody bollocking bastard!' I shouted as I tripped. Searing pain tore through my face.

Pulling myself into a sitting position, I… *Wait, why am I on the floor?* I pressed my hand to my face and squinted up at the glass. Not glass. Transparent aluminium. Or something. Whatever.

I was seeing stars. Except something was off. The stars weren't normally in the room with me. I squinted at the window. *Where'd all that red paint come from? Who paints a window anyway?*

Pain bit into my face a second time and I reached up to put a hand to my nose. All at once, I tasted blood, felt warm liquid down my front, and saw my hand coated in red. 'Wha' habbuh?'

Spock – ever the dutiful German shepherd – was at my

side, sniffing my face. 'Lem okay?' She licked the blood from my hand. *Gross.*

'We have dropped out of warp,' said Holly, my personal AI and universal translator.

'Eh wuv a wewowica kwesha.' I put a hand to my lip. Blood flowed freely through my fingers.

'Please repeat that,' replied my idiot chatbot of an AI.

Except I wouldn't be pronouncing the words *rhetorical* or *question* for a while. I hobbled to the loo to rinse my mouth out. Two and a half teeth fell into the sink. My teeth! And I was pretty sure my nose hadn't been … there. It was distinctly to the left of where it had been the last time I looked. I grabbed a towel to stem the bleeding. Biting down on it, I ducked to get a good look in the mirror. Maybe someday we'd get human-height mirrors, but probably not today. I peeled the edge of the towel carefully away just enough to get a look at what was happening.

In addition to my nose's spontaneous relocation, my bottom lip was split and a red stain marred the soft cotton-like towel. It was still spreading. The front and sleeves of my hoodie – my original Earth-made hoodie – were coated in blood.

'Hawwuh, kuh kah suh fuh meh, puzh?' As in, *Holly, can you call someone for me, please?*

'Please repeat the question,' said Holly unhelpfully.

Great. How am I supposed to call for help when I can't bloody speak properly? The pun left me biting back a chuckle that would undoubtedly hurt like a bastard. I stepped back into the main room, holding the towel to my face with one hand and fumbling my phone with the other, trying to text someone for help. Only the device was slick with blood and impossible to hold onto.

Spock ran over and sniffed at my face. She pushed me

backwards until I landed on my arse on the sofa, then stood astride me, licking my face. 'Lem broken.'

The door whooshed open, admitting both BB and Henry.

'What have you done to the ship, sandwich?' said the robot. 'And why is your ducking user interface leaking?'

Still standing over me, Spock turned. In doing so, her paw dug into me – it felt like she was trying to push all the way through to my kidney. 'Lem broken,' she repeated over the sound of my cries.

BB clucked her beak as she prodded at me. 'Oh dear, Lem! What have you done to yourself? Is your body trying to kill you again?'

'Whuh oo do hee?' That time I was nearly coherent, I was sure of it. I looked up at the doc so she could get a look at me.

'I've no idea what you just said.' The overhead lights in the room came on as BB took the towel from my hand and peeled it back slowly so she could inspect my injury. 'But if you're asking what I'm doing here, the answer is that Spock called me. She said it was a medical emergency. If you're asking how bad it is … well, you'll live. Probably. I assume. But we should get you to the medlab so I can patch you up. And, Henry' – BB looked over my shoulder – 'we'll need you to print a replica of some of Lem's mouth bones.'

Henry's smooth, posh tones responded. 'You don't think maybe I should investigate why the bollarding ship suddenly came to a complete halt in the middle of frolicking nowhere, do you?'

'Emergency! Wake everyone.' Spock's voice was calm but authoritative.

The lights flashed purple. 'Mauve alert,' said Holly in my ear. 'All hands to Ten Backwards. Mauve alert.'

Did Spock really just put the Teapot *into some sort of alert mode? Because I bonked my noggin?*

Henry wheeled over to where I was sitting. Her feature-less blue cylinder glowed purple in the flashing alarm lights. 'What did you do to make us drop out of clucking warp like that, anyway, meatsack?'

I jerked my face out of BB's talon, sending another spurt of blood down my chest. 'Bee?'

BB flapped one wing in Henry's direction, warning her to back off. 'Lem will answer your questions just as soon as I've patched her up.'

We headed for the lift, meeting Bexley and Aurora as they exited. Bexley's normally lustrous, wavy blond mane stood up in every direction. Aurora was a nebulous cloud of sentient rainbow-hued glitter gas. Depending on her mood or emotions, certain colours rose to prominence or receded. Right then, her rainbow hues had given way to a mix of turquoise and pale blue glitter gas – worry and curiosity.

Bexley rubbed her eyes with the back of one of her hooves. 'What's going on? Why have we stopped—' Her already large eyes opened even larger – making her look like a My Little Pony doll. 'Holy crap, Lem! What happened to your face? Are you leaking? What's that red fluid? Is that ichor? Oh! Is it lymph?'

BB guided me into the lift. 'Let me deal with my patient. We'll return as soon as I've patched her up. Henry's in Ten Backwards. She'll tell you what she knows. We'll join you in a bit.' Spock followed us into the lift.

'Bib ou pine bye peeve?' I should have known better than to try to ask if she'd found my teeth.

BB squinted at me. 'I can't tell whether you've suffered a brain injury that's making you delirious or if your injuries are preventing you from speaking coherently. Either way, I suggest you stop trying to talk for the time being. I'll get your lip sewn up and give you an injection to bring the swelling back down and then we can check your cognitive abilities.'

Still holding the towel to my face, I nodded.

'Good.' She patted my arm.

When we got to the medlab, BB got me positioned on a chair and shone a light in my face as she waved something like a tricorder over me.

She studied the readings for a moment before speaking. 'How the devil did you manage this, Lem? Your nose is broken, your lip is torn open, two of your mouth bones are entirely missing, and another is chipped.'

I didn't even try to answer as she left me and went to rummage around in a cupboard, before spending a few minutes doing things I couldn't see. Before long, she wheeled over a small tray with a variety of bizarre implements. The first thing she picked up looked like a pen. 'This is a hypospray. I've loaded it with a substance that will temporarily block pain sensations in' – she waved a taloned hand at my bust and bloody face – 'your beak region.'

Before Spock would let her work, she insisted on sniffing the implement. Apparently satisfied, she lay down next to me.

BB placed the pen to my jaw and waved it around, covering every inch of my face. Everywhere the pen-thing moved, my pain dropped away instantly. Then she told me to open up, and she repeated the process inside my mouth. I hadn't even had time to think about how much my face hurt – until it didn't.

Once she was happy with the results, she hefted a whirring tool about the size of a can of beer. 'This one will realign your beak and stitch up the torn bits of flesh. Now, hold very still please. It shouldn't hurt but you may feel a bit of pressure.'

Instead of sniffing this one, Spock whimpered and backed away.

She needn't have worried. There was no pain – not once the painkiller pen had done its magic. BB was right, though. Having your nose unbroken and your lip sewn back together using – I don't know – ultrasonic frequencies or nanoparticles or whatever… It feels strange. If you've never been through it, I don't know how to describe it to you other than to say it's just plain weird.

Once she finished repairing the torn flesh, BB stood back up and studied my face. 'I must say, this bloating makes you look a lot smoother. Well, that is, we could make it permanent if you liked.'

'Boating?' I parroted. Not having gaping holes in my face or blood streaming everywhere made my words a bit closer to what I was trying to say –

'Marine transport? Oh dear. Maybe you are delirious.'

– but apparently not close enough.

Waving both hands at my face, I tried again. 'Bwoa – No, newer mine.'

'A modern site of excavation?'

I brought my fists to my face and started over again. 'Can ou fif it?'

BB cocked her to one side. 'My translator says there's a sixty-three per cent chance you're asking if I can fix it.'

I made a noise that sounded nothing like the word 'yes'. Trying to speak coherently with your face and tongue swollen to double their normal size was difficult enough without having to worry about sibilants.

BB picked up something that looked like a pen and waved it. 'You're in luck. This will reduce the inflammation.'

As before, she waved it around my face and in my mouth – once Spock had inspected the thingamy. 'Now, this drug doesn't work as quickly as the other,' BB said. 'But in a minute or so, you should feel the swelling start to come down. I'll tidy up and, by the time I'm done, you should notice a difference. Then we'll do a quick scan to ensure you're functioning normally.'

A little more than half an hour later, the three of us returned to Ten Backwards. After fixing the damage and running a few scans, BB helped me clean myself. We'd even stopped by my quarters so I could change into a clean jumper. My swelling was down and my pain was gone. The teeth would have to wait. At least I could speak again – now with added lisp thanks to the missing teeth.

BB crossed the room and climbed up onto her perch.

'Hey!' Bexley ran over and cupped her hooves around my jaw. 'Oh my gosh. Are you okay, Lem? What happened? Was it related to the other ship?' She sniffed at my face carefully.

For a moment, I just stood there gawping at her, unsure of how to explain or where to start. 'Uvva ship?' The words felt strange in my teeth-reduced mouth.

Spock padded over to the sofa and climbed up, where her abandoned brain lay. I'd bought the pink plush squeaky toy for her at a science fiction convention in London the day before we met at a dog shelter. It was her most treasured possession – also her only possession. Well, she also had her translator. She curled up on the sofa, brain clutched between her front paws.

'Yes, another ship,' said Henry. 'That jolt you felt when the warp drive cut out was the deflector fields of the two ships colliding.'

My hands fell slack by my side. 'We crashed into another ship?'

'We look ficus dead to you, pancake?' Henry turned in impatient circles.

'Yeah, no, for sure.' Bexley brushed her forelock down over her long, horsey nose. 'If our deflector shields weren't working, we totally would have crashed. Basically, we have these, like, sensors and fields of repellent energy that surround our ship. When the sensors detect any matter in our path, the shields sort of like… well, you know.'

I didn't know. But now seemed the wrong time to ask for a science lesson. And I knew the result well enough.

Aurora floated across the room to her spouse, her nebulous edges gently ruffling BB's feathers. 'Henry's just been explaining it all to us. No one's quite sure yet why we fell out of warp, but when we did, we came very close to a derelict vessel.'

Bexley grabbed my hand and dragged me to the sofa. I was too tired to resist. 'A mostly derelict ship. *Mostly* being the key word. It's way warmer than it ought to be. Like, way above the freezing point of air – barely even below the freezing point of water. Anyways, it's so exciting. Oh, and it looks like it might have an atmosphere.'

'Okay, that's … weird. Are there any life signs on board?' I could hear myself mispronouncing my Rs, Ss and THs. I hoped everyone's translators could parse my words more easily than they had managed earlier.

Bexley tilted her head and BB stopped preening herself. Both of them looked at me. If I couldn't talk to anyone until I got my teeth fixed, this was going to be a problem.

'Life signs?' Bexley repeated.

So they *could* understand me. 'Yeah, are we picking up any … life…' I ran my hand over the back of my neck. 'That's not a thing we can do, is it? Right, so what should we do? We should call the space police, yeah?'

'Well, we would do.' Henry spun her wheels. 'Except our ansible went down at the same time as our engines.'

I pulled my knees up to my chin, careful not to make contact with my damaged lip. 'So, now we're dead in the water, floating next to a maybe-derelict spaceship. Have I got that right?'

Bexley tossed her mane over her shoulders. 'What? We're not dead. You know that, right?'

'And no one's mentioned any water.' BB stroked her chin. 'Are you sure you didn't injure your brain when you fell? Maybe we need to run some more tests.'

2 / WELL, THAT
WAS UNEXPECTED

One metaphor-clarification and ten minutes later, I dropped into the human-sized chair in the mess hall. Although the pain was still absent, I felt like I needed a good, long nap. But I wasn't going to get one. Not yet, anyways.

Bexley placed two mugs on the table before giving me a careful hug. 'I don't want to, like, re-injure you. I had a look at the – you know – bodily fluids from Ten Backwards. Holy crap, was that a mess! Like, how many holes were you leaking from? It was all over the window and floor. And the bathroom looked like someone had been popping bananas without a— Anyways, never mind. All that matters is your health. How are you now? I made you a big cup of helbru because I figured you'd probably need some energy.'

Spock danced over to where Aurora hovered, guiding the rolling tray into the room. 'Feed Spock?'

Aurora allowed a portion of herself to stretch out and wave through Spock's ears, tickling her. 'Soon, darling.'

Bexley released me and cantered back across the room to fetch the bowls of food from Aurora's tray. 'Don't worry, Spock. Aurora's got you covered.' She delivered one bowl to

Spock, one to me, and set the final one down next to her own mug.

I wrapped my hands around my large, bowl-shaped mug and let the warmth infuse into me. Helbru was the nearest thing I'd found to coffee. It was bright purple and tasted of Marmite and flowers. Basically, it was pretty gross and nothing like coffee. But at least it had a mild stimulant effect.

'Cheers, Bex. If I have to stay awake, I'm going to need this.' Although I could feel the heat of the mug through my hands, the steam didn't warm my face. Nor did I feel the condensation that was almost certainly gathering, presumably due to the drugs BB had given me.

I took a long gulp from the mug. I can't say I savoured the taste, but I like to imagine I could feel the little buzz of energy slowly spread through me. 'What's the plan? I take it we're intending to board the, er —'

'—the maybe- maybe-not abandoned craft?' Bexley shovelled a spoonful of nutrient porridge into her big horsey mouth. From here, it smelt sort of like lemongrass. 'Yeah, no, for sure. Soon as we finish breakfast.'

Resting my hand on the lid of my bowl, I wondered what Aurora had in store for me. Nutrient porridge – always nutrient porridge – but how would she flavour it today? I wasn't sure I had the energy for any of her more unusual flavour combinations.

Bexley swallowed, then stuck her spoon back in the bowl. 'Or is this more of a midnight snack? What time is it anyways? I was sound asleep when I got the alert – haven't even had a chance to stop and check what time it is. But I'm still really— Anyways, whatever. What time is it?'

Glancing at my watch, I yawned. 'Quarter past five. Guess that makes this an early breakfast.' I lifted the lid off the dish in front of me and braced for what I might find.

Nutrient porridge could be flavoured like anything at all – but it was still going to have the texture and appearance of a slightly grey risotto. Taking a careful sniff, I grimaced. 'Is that…?'

Aurora glided over to where we were sat. 'It's beer. It's a flavour you had saved as a favourite, yet according to my records you've not had it once in the time you've been on the ship.'

Beer. Beer-flavoured nutrient porridge. Ah well. Had to eat something. I stifled a chuckle and scooped a spoonful of it into my mouth.

———

Half an hour later, Spock, Bexley, and I boarded the other ship. Spock was our Director of Security, so it was her job to go. And where she went, I generally followed. Bexley was our mechanic. She wanted to see what, if anything, they had that we might be able to use to make repairs to get us moving.

The other ship was small compared to most deep-space vessels – not even the size of a London bus. Only our long-range comms were down, so we'd tried hailing them. But to no avail. Once we'd docked with it, we were able to test the atmosphere. It was breathable, though well below freezing.

I stepped through the docking bay door into the cold, dark ship and halted. The only light in the space came from our head-torches. 'I've got a bad feeling about this.'

Bexley touched my elbow as she squeezed past me, wearing a sort of insulated blanket-poncho. 'Oh, don't be such a spoilsport. Where's your sense of adventure? Besides, what if they need our help? They might be lost or starving or broken down.'

I grimaced. 'Then why didn't they answer when we tried

to contact them?' Spock pushed past me and ran to the end of the hall and up a curving ramp. Presumably there was another deck directly above the one we'd entered on. 'Hey, come back here. We should stick together. You don't know what's up there.'

It was too late, of course. Both Spock and Bexley were long gone – out of my line of sight.

Grumbling about health and safety, I shivered and dug my hands into the front pocket of my own blanket-poncho as I lumbered after them in the frigid darkness. I removed my hands from the warmth of the coat just long enough to pull the hood up over my long, blond ponytail.

The light from my head-torch caught a glimpse of Spock chasing something into a corner.

I heard, rather than saw, Spock yip and then whimper. Bracing myself on the edge of the wall, I spun around the corner and crashed into her as she sped back out of the room she'd only just entered.

'Spock, what happened? Where are you going?'

'Spock scare.' The clicking of her claws on the floor receded swiftly into the distance.

I looked around the room I'd entered. It seemed to be set up as sleeping quarters – a bed, small desk, and knick-knacks on a shelf above the desk. 'What? Why are you scared, you silly beast? There's nothing here.'

Just as I was about to head out to continue my exploration of the ship, I heard a tiny squeak from under the bed. 'What on Earth?'

'Please repeat the question,' said Holly.

'Never mind. I'm talking to myself.' You'd think the thing would learn.

I bent down, trying to find where the noise came from. 'Is it a bleeping alarm clock? A burglar alarm? A freezer door left open – I suppose that would explain the temperature, at least.' When my headlamp cast its glow in the small, dim space, my jaw hit the floor. Figuratively. The doc had given me a stern warning not to go injuring myself any further while my face healed.

'What? I mean, hello. Er, you're safe now. I promise we won't hurt you. Come here.' I reached out slowly, not wanting to spook the tiny ball of fluff in front of me. The creature sniffed my hand, then licked it. Lifting my other hand – the one with my watch – to my face, I whispered, 'Holly, can you tell Bexley to come here, please? But quietly. Tell her I've found something and I don't want to spook it. Or her. I'm not sure yet.'

Nothing.

'Holly?'

'Are you speaking to me this time, Lem?' came the idiot response.

'Yes, Holly.' I kept my voice as soft as I could. 'That's why I said your name, you—' Inhaling slowly, I bit my lip – not that I could feel it. Probably shouldn't do that right now – might tear the stitches. 'Can you ask Bexley to come here, please? But quietly.'

'Of course, Lem.'

The creature under the bed crept forwards. It – or she – shivered with each painfully slow step. 'Help?'

Well, that settled it.

Thanks to a snap decision I made on my very first day in space, all sapient beings are *she* – biologic or inorganic, corporeal, gestalt, or disembodied. Everyone.

In a galaxy where gender is meaningless and where each species has its own take on the sexes, there are two singular third-person pronouns: she and it. *Its* don't speak. *It* is an inanimate object or a non-sapient being. If someone is capable of speech, she's a she. It could just as easily have been they. If I were a cis-het man, I'd be calling everyone he. But I'm not. So here we are.

'Help?' the tiny fluffball pleaded again.

'Hiya.' I whispered with as much reassuring cheerfulness as I could muster. 'Of course we'll help you. Come here. You're safe, I promise.' I beckoned her closer.

The little being took two very shaky steps out from under the bed just as Bexley's voice reached us. 'Hey, Lem. You're never going to guess what I found. It's so amazingly cool. Oh my gosh, I'm reminded of this time my friend and I took one of my dad's shuttles out when I was a teenager. She told us not to but you know what kids are like. So anyways we — Oh!'

As Bexley came around the corner, the puppy – for that's exactly what my new friend appeared to be – climbed into my lap.

'What do you have here? Hi.' Bexley leant over me and peered at my little friend. 'You look like a baby version of Spock.' She sniffed. 'You smell like her, too. Not that that's a bad thing, obviously. I love Spock's smell. It's sort of soft and fuzzy – you know, like a lemon-melon.'

I wondered if the puppy had a translator; I couldn't see one. Without it, she could talk to us, but she'd have no clue what we said to her. I stroked her icy fur. Beneath it, she was skin and bones.

'Oh my gosh, Lem.' Bexley laid a hoof on my shoulder. 'I don't get it. How is there a baby on this ship? *Why* is there a baby?'

'Not a Scooby, mate.' I stroked the puppy's thick fur and studied her. She really did look like a mini-Spock: a German shepherd puppy – maybe a couple months of age. 'How have you survived out here all alone, little one? What have you been eating?'

The puppy crept off my lap. She seemed to gain confidence as she moved and by the time she got to the door, she was practically scampering.

Bexley nickered anxiously. 'And what's she been drinking? It's below freezing in here.'

Huh. 'I guess we'd better follow her and find out.'

We chased the wayward puppy, taking care to step softly. There was no sign of Spock. 'Hey, Holly – where's Spock?'

The puppy rounded the corner into the next room along – Bexley and me hot on her heels.

'Spock is aboard the *Teapot*, in the cargo hold,' replied Holly.

'What, why?' The room the puppy had led us to looked like a kitchen or galley. A bag of some kind of food was torn open – chewed open by the look of it. The contents, now spread across the floor, were almost entirely gone.

'Would you like me to contact her to ask?' said Holly.

The puppy licked weakly at the remnants of the food, her tiny body looking so frail and helpless. 'What? Ask who what? Oh, you mean Spock? No, it's okay. I'll talk to her soon. But can you please tell BB that we're going to need her in the medlab, though? Pronto.' I looked at Bexley. 'Oh, I forgot. What'd you find?'

Bexley waved her hooves. 'Never mind. I'll tell you about that after. You need to get the puppy to BB. She doesn't look very well.'

I nodded and looked down at my new little charge on the floor. She wobbled on her feet as she licked the empty bag of food. 'Right, friend. Let's get you to the Doc. She'll have you right as rain in no time.' I scooped her up – she weighed nothing – and headed for the docking bay. Looking back over my shoulder, I added, 'Bexley, I'll see you in a bit, yeah?'

Bexley was already wandering off. 'Yeah, no worries. I still have to find the engine room.'

The poor little thing was shivering and panting in my arms. Mind you, I was shivering too. The temperature in the derelict ship – though practically balmy compared to what it should have been, what with floating dead in space and all – was below freezing. My little friend felt so weak. Holding her to my chest, I raced through the alien ship and back through the door to the warmth of the *Teapot*.

3 / PUPPY POWER!

Spock waited for me just inside the door. 'Lem! Lem come back!' She sniffed the air and repeatedly nosed me as she followed me to the lift. 'Lem got puppy? Why puppy? Who puppy? How puppy?' I'd never heard her speak so much all at once.

The lift door opened and I shivered as we all got in. 'Medlab, please.' The lift began to move. Consciously, I knew it was one level down from the deck where the docking bay was to the medlab and guest accommodations. Still, the motion in a lift always felt weirdly directionless – probably something to do with the artificial gravity, but I doubt I'll ever know for certain.

Still clutching the puppy to my chest with one hand, I used the other to rub my arm in a desperate attempt to thaw myself out.

When the door opened again, BB was waiting for us. She lifted her vividly coloured wings in greeting. 'Lem, what's wrong? What's happened? Did you hurt yourself again? Is Spock okay?' She pulled herself up to her full height as she followed us down the corridor, trying to peer around my shoulder as we moved. 'Oh my! What have you here? Who is this?'

The door to the medlab whooshed open and I ducked in. 'Have you got an incubator? She needs to be warmed up.'

BB clucked. 'You haven't even let me see the patient.' She tried to get a closer look. 'What makes you think her temperature is insufficient?'

Spock leapt onto the one bed in the room.

My jaw clamped shut as I forced myself to swallow down my stress for the puppy's sake. *Why on Earth did Spock have to pick now to play silly beggars*? 'No, Spock. You're not the patient. This little puppy is.'

But Spock was way ahead of me. As always. I should have known. She curled her body into a sort of C-shape on the bed. 'Give puppy. Spock warm.' She was offering to comfort the tiny creature with her own body – just like she'd do if she had puppies of her own.

I set my little bundle down by Spock's belly. The puppy nuzzled into the warmth. Spock, bless her, actually licked the wretched thing. My heart almost melted – even though I was still shivering as my body re-adjusted to the *Teapot*'s temperature.

I'd have to come up with a name for her at some point – even if she already had a name for herself or we eventually found her people.

See, that was the thing with life in outer space: some things just don't translate. Like names. Take Bexley, for example. Her name for herself sounded like a paperback tumbling down a flight of stairs. But the sound of a *hardcover* book falling down the same flight of stairs? Well, that was her people's word for pornographic soup. Bexley found the similarity hilarious.

I could only barely hear the difference – at least half her language was below the minimum frequency I could hear. And I had absolutely no hope of ever pronouncing the difference. And I certainly wasn't going to call her Pornographic Soup.

And that's why universal translators didn't even try to translate names. Instead, we all assigned names of our own choosing to everyone we met and our AIs would remember and adapt accordingly. And the other person's AI would translate my name for her into whatever she wanted to be called.

BB shoved me gently aside so she could examine her newest patient. She moved deftly, working around Spock. As she did so, I had my first proper chance to study the creature.

'Oh my days! How can this be? By all appearances, this is an actual German shepherd puppy. I mean, I'm not exactly a puppy expert – Spock was more than a year old when I got her.' I squatted low to get a better look. 'But I'd guess she might be around two or three months old. Very much in the infancy range. I don't even think they start toilet training until around five months.'

How was there an abandoned puppy aboard a derelict ship in deep space? *Why* was there a puppy in outer space? *Who* would abandon a puppy on a spaceship? How long had she been there on her own? 'What the hell is happening?'

BB clucked and stood upright. She walked to the corner and removed a small bowl from a cupboard, filling it with water at the sink. 'Well, I don't know for certain, but it does appear we have a juvenile of a species that is either the same as Spock or uncannily similar. From my understanding of Spock's physiology and from the circumstances of her discovery, I'd say our new friend is probably dehydrated and a bit malnourished. But she's basically healthy – more or less.' She held the bowl for the puppy, who lapped it all up.

BB stroked her patient with one taloned hand. 'Why don't we take our little patient to the kitchen to get her some breakfast?'

Spock stood up on the bed, almost knocking the puppy to the floor. 'Feed Spock?'

Okay, so maybe she wasn't quite ready for a 'Foster Parent of the Year' award.

I scooped the puppy up in my arms – she felt warmer now than she had a few minutes ago. 'Let's get you something to eat, little one.' Narrowing my eyes at Spock, I added, 'And no, you had your breakfast before we boarded the other ship, remember?'

Spock's ears and jaw dipped. 'No. Spock not eat. Hungry.'

The universal translator may have allowed us to speak to one another, but it didn't change her nature.

'Of course you are. But I assure you, you've had sufficient food.'

Her tail gave a sad little wag. 'No. Starving.'

I put my free hand on my hip and raised my eyebrow.

'Feed puppy?' The puppy's little tail tickled me as she thumped it against my chest.

'Oh, hang on.' I looked up at BB. 'Shouldn't we stop to get her a translator on the way to the kitchen?'

As we walked towards the lift, BB said, 'Our little guest is too young for a translator. Her thoughts aren't yet mature. She needs to gain the ability to use language – any language – in order for the translator to have a framework to build on.'

I pressed the button to call the lift. 'But I can understand her.' Chewing my lower lip, I considered the past few minutes. 'At least, *sometimes* I can.'

BB tilted her head. 'Occasionally, I forget you didn't grow up in a world where universal translators are commonplace.' The lift whooshed open and we all stepped in. 'Level zero. Hatchlings communicate their needs very clearly – well, some of the time, at any rate – and your translator picks up on that. But all they understand are their own immediate needs. A translator wouldn't be able to communicate your words to them because, first of all, they don't understand language. And secondly, they don't understand the complex concepts we use language to convey.'

As the lift door opened on the *Teapot*'s lowest deck, Holly announced a call from Bexley.

I stepped out into the hallway. 'Hey, Bexley.'

'Oh, my gosh,' squealed Bexley. 'You're never going to believe what I just found. Like, seriously, never in a million years. I mean, this is so far beyond what I was expecting to find that — Anyways, whatever. Just go on, guess!'

BB stroked her beak with a small, taloned hand. 'Is it someone in a stasis pod?'

'No, it's a— Wait, how did you know that?' Bexley's disembodied voice paused while she – presumably – looked around. 'Henry and Aurora are both still here with me. How'd you know that?'

I stepped into the kitchen and headed for the dish cupboard. 'Not that I'm an expert or anything but, well, that ship has to have got here somehow.' I set a bowl in the food dispenser.

BB paused in the doorway. 'Does the person in the pod appear to be alive?'

'Totally,' said Bexley. 'Well, I mean, she's not deteriorated or anything. So, like, I guess so. Probably. I'm not a doctor, but—'

'No, dear, you are definitely not.' BB stroked the puppy's face once more.

'Yeah, no, for sure. The lights on the pod are blinking purple, though.'

'That's not a good sign.' BB ground her beak. 'I'll grab my medkit and be with you in a moment.'

'Thanks, Doc,' said Bexley. 'I'll see you when you get here.'

BB paused in the doorway. 'May I suggest you prepare food based on Spock's profile? Though you'll probably want to water it down for her. It's not perfect – but it'll have to do for right now. Oh, and I'd imagine it should be lukewarm.'

'Cheers, Doc.' I nodded at her. 'You go help the others. Spock and I have this one.' As BB left, I stared at the dispenser's screen. Spock's favourite was sweet potato vindaloo. Well, nutrient porridge flavoured like vindaloo. I looked down at the puppy in my arms. 'But you probably want more of a bland brekkie, don't you?'

Once I'd set the puppy on the floor, I tapped out an instruction: the same nutrient profile as Spock, but without flavour. The food dispenser spat out a pink powder followed by steaming water. It didn't seem fair to feed the puppy and give Spock nothing – she wouldn't understand that. So I set about prepping Spock a very small meal.

Both dogs were drooling and underfoot as I swapped out the porridge for an empty bowl and entered the order for Spock's little treat. While the machine made that one, I stirred the contents of the first.

The puppy climbed onto my shoe and pawed at my tights. 'Ow!' I shoved her gently aside. 'Those claws of yours are sharp … you. Whatever your name is.' The dogs followed me – in so far as clambering along under my feet can be said to be following – through the door to the mess hall. I set both bowls on the floor.

The puppy tried to eat Spock's food, so I lifted her out of the way and placed her back in front of her own. I sat on the floor and held the bowl for her. 'You really do look like a baby Spock.'

I considered the matter and stroked her fluffy puppy fur as she wolfed down her food. 'I think I'll call you Scrappy.'

4 / HOW MUCH MESS CAN
ONE PUPPY MAKE?

Scrappy licked her bowl clean in approximately the time it took me to blink. She followed this by climbing into my lap and trying to tip my mug onto herself. 'Hey! No. This one's mine. It's not my fault you ate yours so quickly.'

She was undeterred and carried on trying to grab at my helbru.

'And besides, the last thing you need is a stimulant.' I took another sip of the brew.

The lounge door slid open, letting Bexley and Aurora walk in. Or rather, one walked and one floated. The brief lapse in my attention was enough for Scrappy to succeed in knocking my mug from my hands, dumping the remaining contents onto my lap. 'No!'

Fortunately, the helbru hadn't been hot any longer. Warm, but not hot. Both my skirt and my T-shirt were covered in a warm, sticky mess – which quickly turned into a cold, sticky mess. Ugh. As early as it was, this was already my second outfit of the day. Or was it my third?

And let's not even mention my blood-soaked hoodie.

'Oh dear,' said Aurora. 'You should be more careful.

Your blanket armour will require laundering.' That was the closest translation for clothes we'd come up with. Armour and blankets both seemed to be fairly common concepts – or at least common enough that most species had words for them. But clothes were rare. The idea that people would need to cover themselves for reasons of practicality and/or decency was, well, alien to most species in the Galactic Union.

Bexley looked perplexed. 'That was weird. I had to tell the door to open. Usually, it opens itself automatically when anyone approaches it. I'll have a look at the mechanism.' She popped open the control panel next to the door and studied the inner workings.

Looking up, I made a face that was half chuckle and half grimace. 'Sorry, that was me. I set it to require a command from one of the *Teapot* crew. I don't want Scrappy wandering off. I've already had to clean the floor three times – and you don't want to know about my jumper.'

I waved towards the growing pile in the far corner of the room. 'Don't look over there. Aurora's right – I really do need to do laundry. As well as all this' – I motioned at the mess down my front – 'my jumper and about a dozen cleaning cloths all need to go in the wash. Anyway, about the doors... No one wants to deal with surprise puppy messes. Plus, I'm not sure what age the chewing starts.'

'Chewing?' Bexley pulled a sceptical face as she picked Scrappy up and held her in front of herself. 'You wouldn't bite me – would you, little one? You're far too fluffy and adorab— Ow!' Scrappy chomped down on Bexley's nose. 'Okay, I take that back. Those are some sharp little teeth you've got there, pal. I can see you're really proud of them.' She set the puppy back down on the floor and pressed her hoof to her nose.

The puppy scampered over to Aurora and sniffed her, then promptly widdled … er … in her.

I yanked on my hair and let out a small and entirely dainty shriek. 'Gah! No, Scrappy. No, you mustn't wee on anyone. I'm so sorry, Aurora.' I scrambled to the kitchen to grab yet another cloth.

When I had cleaned up the mess, I asked, 'So what happened with the person in the stasis pod?'

At that moment, Aurora was mainly royal blue – indicating amusement. But small pockets of her seemed to disappear entirely. I'd begun to suspect this implied colours outside the human visual range. I had no idea how many of her mood-ring colours I couldn't actually see.

Her voice was the auditory equivalent of buttered velvet. 'We brought the pod aboard and took it to the medlab. BB's running some checks and then she's going to wake the occupant up.'

Bexley got down on all fours and scampered about, chasing the puppy playfully. 'That's what we came to tell you, Lem. We thought Scrappy would probably want to see her friend again.'

'Oh.' I wasn't sure why my heart fell at the thought of handing Scrappy back. After all, she wasn't ours to keep. And she was proving to be way more work than I wanted to commit to. I hadn't done this much laundry since that time we'd visited a planet with mud storms.

Still.

'That's … good. I'm sure you're excited to get your person back, aren't you?'

Scrappy ran from Bexley to me, licked my nose, then lapped twice around the room. She hurled herself harshly into Spock's lap, then turned herself around a couple of times before flopping down indignantly against Spock's belly.

Brushing down my clothes, I determined to ignore the small wet patch on my elbow. I dropped onto the sofa and looked at Bexley. 'So, do we have any idea what happened yet? And what we're going to do?'

'Yeah, so...' She plunked down onto her haunches right there on the floor. 'I talked to Henry while we were on our way down here. We hit a pocket of transwarp null space – which is presumably also what happened to the other ship as well. I guess. I don't know. Maybe. Anyways, it knocked us out of warp, drained our dilithium crystals, and fried our ansible.'

Thank figurative mode for that whopper of an explanation. 'Crap. So, we're stuck? What are we going to do? We can't go anywhere, can't call for help.' I frowned and chewed on my lip. 'Also, that really smells like a trap, doesn't it?'

Aurora glowed pale blue. 'I haven't noticed an odour. Not that I'd know what a trap smelt like. What makes you think it could be a trap? What sort of trap?'

I glanced over at the puppy, curled up next to Spock, snoring happily. 'I don't know. Space pirates? Are there space pirates – is that a thing? Because this would seem like a really handy way to rob ships – don't you think?'

'I suppose,' said Aurora. 'That makes a certain kind of sense.'

'Huh.' Bexley breathed out noisily as she studied me. 'Your people sure come up with some interesting ideas.' She crossed the room and joined me on the sofa.

Thinking about all the various ways humans deceived and connived, I had to agree with her.

Bexley pushed her forelock down over her long nose, covering the stump of a unicorn horn. It was a nervous habit. Even now that everyone knew she was a unicorn – pretty much everyone in the galaxy knew thanks to a well-publicised trial a few months before. Even though she knew on a conscious level that unicornism wasn't anything to be ashamed of, she still lived with a lot of residual shame.

'It's lucky we had a bit of unobtainium … stashed away. Well, I mean … you know.' She waved at her face. Unicorn horns were infused with the substance that recrystallised our dilithium and allowed us to travel faster than light speed. I didn't even begin to understand the science – and part of me figured it was more fun that way. The shavings of her horn could buy us enough *voom* to go further than we could using our sub-light engines. Without the first clue how it worked, I was just along for the ride. However it worked, it worked.

For a long time, I was the only one who knew about Bexley's secret superpower. Or rather, Bexley and I *thought* I was the only one who knew. Her culture viewed unicorns as some sort of underclass – less than people. I was the only one she'd told, but when her family had another baby with a different form of skeledivergence – pegacism – we'd all been caught up in a court case that made front-page news across the galaxy.

'We're so lucky to have you, Bexley.' I wrapped my arm around her.

'We're *always* lucky to have you, Bexley,' said Aurora. 'You bring so much joy to this crew. But I agree with Lem, in situations like this, your presence is especially fortu—'

The lounge doors whooshed open and Henry wheeled in. 'What's up, sandwiches?'

'Good morning, Henry.' Aurora glided smoothly across the room. 'We were just saying how lucky we are that Bexley's able to provide us with an alternative source of unobtainium.'

Henry harrumphed.

'When I was held captive by the bunnyboos,' Aurora said,

'they always told me it was too perishable to carry stocks of, so we had to be cautious never to run out. If this had happened when they were running the ship, I'm not sure what they'd have done.'

Bexley shrugged – a human gesture she'd picked up from me – and opted to play with the puppy instead of commenting.

'For a change, the pluckers weren't wrong. Unobtanium starts losing effectiveness as soon as it's manufactured. You'd have to be a special kind of incompetent' – Henry stabbed something like a spanner in my direction – 'to buy unobtainium you didn't need to use immediately.'

Bexley stood. 'Apparently, I'm nothing but a fuel source to you!' She bolted from the room.

Scooping the puppy into my arms, I followed her. 'I'll make sure she's okay. She knows we love her for who she is.' Spock trailed after me as I ran down the hall. The engine room was empty when we got there – but the little purple light next to the door in the far corner told me the loo was occupied. I set the main door to require a voice command then set the puppy down. I sat with my back to the wall. Both dogs curled up next to me as we waited for Bexley to finish.

5 / SHE'S DEAD, JIM

After a couple of minutes, the toilet door slid open and Bexley emerged. She held a cup carefully in front of herself and gave a shy smile.

'I figured you'd be here.' I tilted my head sympathetically. After all, I knew what it was like to assume people couldn't – or wouldn't – accept you. 'You get that everyone loves you, right? I mean, we love you for who you are, not just for … you know.' I motioned towards the cup she held.

Scrappy ran to her and jumped up, trying to knock the cup from her hands. When she failed, she tried again and again, hurling herself at Bexley's hooves. After her fourth attempt, I scooped the wriggly ball of fur up in my arms. 'Oi! Cut it out, you. That's not food. And we need it.' She squirmed and twisted, desperately trying to leap from my arms.

With all Scrappy's flailing, Bexley very nearly dropped the cup. But, thankfully, her lightning reflexes meant she caught it with no more than a few grains lost.

Cup held tighter than ever, Bexley walked over to the engine and pulled open the drawer that held the dilithium. 'I know you do.' She set the cup down on top of the engine and knocked the side of her forehead with her left hoof. 'At least, I mostly know – even if I don't always know, you know?' Her right hoof tapped the other side of her forehead.

'I get it.' My heart ached for her. 'Please believe me – no one here judges you. I promise. The crew of the *Teapot* judge people by their actions, not their genetics. Never for things they can't change. And we proved it in court – being a unicorn doesn't make you any less of a person. It really doesn't.' I allowed a smirk to spread across my face. 'What do you think Bungle would say if she heard you talking like this?'

Bungle was one of the equidae we'd met on the sanctuary moon, Lagash. She proudly sported a beautiful horn that was almost a metre high.

From my human perspective, being a unicorn was amazing. It seemed like nothing to be ashamed of. But I knew about hiding a dark secret. When I started presenting more femme – when I asked people to call me *she* – I was terrified that people would reject me. That they wouldn't understand.

And some people did reject me. Some people really didn't get it. One of my childhood best friends told me over and over again that people who were assigned male at birth couldn't be agender *and* use she/her pronouns. She said I had to decide whether I was a trans woman – in which case I could use she/her. Or I could be nonbinary – but then I had to use they/them.

Ridiculous.

Hell, I didn't understand myself most of the time. I wasn't a woman. I wasn't a man. I wasn't any gender. But *she* fit more than *he* ever did.

So I understood Bexley's fear.

As Bexley moved to tip the shavings of her horn into the

drawer, Scrappy jumped up and again tried to knock the cup from her hooves. I stepped in and swooped the rambunctious puppy up. 'Silly puppy. That's still not food.' We joined Bexley to watch the white powder in the drawer form rainbow-hued crystals as the pulverised horn touched it. The process was like magic to me – whether it was achieved via purified unobtainium liquid or unicorn horn.

Her mission accomplished, Bexley flung herself into my arms. 'I'm always on at you to accept yourself. And yet here I am lashing out at people who love me. I know that makes me a hypocrite and a bad person. But I can't help it.'

I held her and rested my chin on the top of her head. One of her pointy ears tickled my ear and the puppy nipped at the corner of my manky T-shirt. 'You're not a bad person. You're amazing – and everyone on this ship knows it.'

I looked down in the drawer. Some of the white powder had crystallised – but not a lot.

Bexley stepped away from me and followed my eyes. 'I should tell Henry. That's enough to get us … well, not far. Maybe a light week or so.'

Scrappy hurled herself out of my arms and threw herself at Spock's belly again. I smiled at them. 'Will that be enough to get us somewhere safe?'

She shrugged. 'We'll have to compare it to the star maps. If we're really lucky, it'll get us to a populated asteroid or a planet. That's pretty unlikely, though. Hopefully, it at least gets us close to an interstellar motorway – so we can send out a sub-light emergency beacon. I'll talk to Henry. Hopefully she can figure out what's in reach and then we'll make our way there.'

I nodded. 'Oh, I suppose we should talk to Scrappy's person too, if she's awake. She might have some additional info or – I don't know – something.' I looked down at myself. 'Though I should probably get cleaned up first.'

'Thank you.' Bexley leant against me. 'For being a good friend, I mean. And for talking me down when I get myself all worked up.'

I stroked her long, blond mane. 'You do the same for me when I freak out. And that happens way more often than you having a moment.'

She grinned and tapped her hooves in the air. 'True.' Pulling herself away from me, she added, 'Right. I'm going to go talk to Henry. Let me know if Scrappy's person tells you anything that might help.' With that, she walked out of the engine room.

I turned to find the two dogs sitting. It was almost like a pair of Russian dolls – small one in front of the larger model. Both stared straight at me. In perfect sync, they tilted their heads to the right.

'What do?' asked Spock.

'Right, you two.' I scooped the puppy up in my arms. 'You're both coming with me while I get changed and then we'll go see what's happening with Scrappy's person.'

We stopped by our quarters so I could put on a clean dress – a pretty one with fabric that was constantly changing patterns – before heading down to the medlab, where we found BB hunched over a stasis pod.

'Hey, BB,' I said. 'Are we all right to come in?'

I expected BB to lift her wings in greeting – but she remained where she was. 'Yes, yes. Of course. Come on in.'

Still cradling Scrappy in my arms, I crossed the small space to join BB. The lid slid shut just as I reached the stasis pod. BB leant over it, resting on her little hands.

Unlike the pods we had, this one was completely opaque. I looked at BB. 'Well, aren't you going to wake her up?'

BB stood upright. 'Hmm… What was that?'

'We should wake her up, no?' I shifted positions as the puppy squirmed in my arms.

'Who?'

I waved a hand at the pod. 'Her.'

'Oh, her!' BB turned to leave the room. 'No, she's dead.'

'What? What happened?' Spock and I had to jog to keep up with her.

BB pressed the button to call the lift. The door opened almost immediately. 'Take me to the kitchen,' she squawked as she strode in.

Spock and I squeezed in as the door slid shut. 'Well?'

BB blinked several times. 'Well … I'm feeling quite peckish, so I thought I'd grab a bite to eat.'

Sometimes people seemed incredibly alien to me. Well, I mean … obviously. But even still. 'Yeah, sure. But aren't you going to tell me what happened to Scrappy's person? I held the puppy aloft as I spoke to make sure she hadn't forgotten our guest.

'I did tell you.' The doors opened. BB looked both ways before turning left, taking the long way round to the kitchen. 'She's dead. Nothing to be done about it.'

'Sure, but what happened?' I caught up with her as she passed the kitchen. 'Hey, I thought you were hungry. Where are you headed now?'

BB stopped and turned to face me. 'Hmm? What's that?'

I stepped up to the kitchen door and it slid open.

BB followed my gesture and walked through the door. 'Yes, sorry. Not sure where my mind is today.' She began opening cupboards seemingly at random, leaving each door open as she moved on to the next.

I looked her in the eye as I removed a bowl from a cupboard she hadn't yet tried and handed it to her. 'Maybe your blood sugar is low – or species equivalent. Actually, I bet it's because you had to get up so early. Let's get you some lunch, eh? You can tell me what happened while you eat.' BB's species needed almost as much sleep as Spock did – which is to say a lot. Having to get up so early always made her a bit funny.

'Yes, that's a wonderful idea. I'll have a … a, er … oh, just get me whatever you're having, would you? There's a dear.' She gave me back the bowl.

I scratched my ear. 'I just ate. But why don't I get you one of your favourites?'

'Sure, I'm sure that will be fine. I'll just go and, er…' She turned in a circle.

I raised a single arm and pointed to the door leading to the crew mess. 'Why don't you go and sit for a bit.' I set Scrappy down on the floor and she scampered off after BB.

Spock looked up at me hopefully. 'Feed Spock?'

I twirled her ear, her fur like velvet in my fingers. 'Sweetie, we had lunch a few minutes ago.'

Her ears pulled back. 'Not feed Spock?'

'Not right now. Why don't you go and look after the puppy for me, please? I'll be through in a minute.' As she followed the other two into the mess hall, I set the empty bowl in the food dispenser then punched in a request for BB's favourite order.

I gave the bowl a stir. Once I had deposited the spoon in the dishwasher, I joined BB in the mess hall. 'There you go, Doc. Millet stew.' I set the bowl on the table and sat down facing her. 'How are you feeling?'

BB's little hands popped out from under her wings. She looked down at the bowl of nutrient porridge then glanced around. 'I'm fine. I'm fine. But there is no spoon. You must have forgotten to bring me one. Would you mind?'

I cocked my head, puzzled. 'A spoon?' BB normally ate by dipping her beak directly into the bowl. I'd never seen her use a spoon.

'Yes, please. Be a dear, would you?'

I went back to the kitchen to grab her some cutlery.

BB spooned the gloopy porridge into her mouth rapidly. In under a minute, the bowl was empty. She grimaced – in so far as a person with a beak instead of a mouth can be said to grimace. 'Not my favourite, but it'll do. I don't suppose you could get me another helping, could you?'

Accepting the proffered bowl, I studied her for a moment.

When I returned with a second portion, I said, 'So what did she die of? Did the stasis pod malfunction? She can't have been in it very long.'

BB swallowed another mouthful. 'How should I know? I'm not—'

The door slid open, cutting off whatever BB was about to say. Bexley burst into the room – full of her characteristic enthusiasm for life, the universe, and everything. 'Okay, so I used what unobtainium we had to recharge the dilithium crystals as much as possible. I mean, I squeezed that unobtainium for all it was worth. It's not very much. And it won't be enough to get us anywhere, like, well, busy. But Henry found a little motorway services station that looks like it's just within our reach.'

She paused and chewed the air for a split second. 'Well, it should be. I mean, no. But we can get close to it and then use the impulse engines for the rest of the journey. If we're really careful in what speed we're travelling at. The most efficient speed is warp 3.7 – for fuel efficiency, I mean. It's obviously not the most... Well, anyways, Henry can get us there.'

I tapped my lip, then thought better of it. There wasn't any pain, but I didn't know if it was still healing on the inside. 'Motorway services? That's good. They should have a comms array, so we can call for help. What does Henry think?'

'She's plotting the course now. We should arrive about four hours from now. My, um, supply was already pretty low. But I bought us an hour in warp and then the rest of the time we'll be travelling at sub-light. We're honestly lucky there was anything this close.' Bexley appeared to notice BB for the first time. 'Oh, hey, Doc. How's your patient?'

BB looked at me, then turned to face Bexley. 'Ah, yes. About that...'

———

Spock, Bexley, and I joined Henry on the bridge as we neared the station. I'd seen dozens of space stations by this point. Some looked like giant wheels, some like giant metal cigars, and others like great hotchpotch thingies composed of thousands of pieces of junk held together with chewing gum and duct tape. And some even looked like giant metal donuts.

But I'd never seen a space station that looked like a donut *shop*.

Honestly, it looked like one of those little drive-through Tim Hortons you get out in the burbs in Canada. Plus a basement. But floating in space.

'With our cupping comms down, we're rocking up without alerting anyone to our situation,' said Henry from her position at the pilot's, er, desk.

'We'll just have to hope for the best. You'd have to figure a place like this would be used to that,' replied Bexley. She and I stood with our noses practically pressed to the not-glass dome. 'That's, like, their whole raison d'être. They set up shop in the middle of nowhere for ships to refuel and restock. And breakdowns in engines or comms equipment must play a significant role in their business model. If I were them, I'd have—' She crouched on all fours and leant over to the right. Waving one hoof at … something, she added, 'Yep, there it is. Around back from our perspective – a mobile response unit. I bet they cover a few light years of space in every direction, rescuing stranded travellers.'

Absently, I stroked Spock's ears. 'Why didn't we— Oh, right. No comms *and* no engines.'

'If we'd sent out a distress signal, it would have eventually reached them,' Bexley said.

'But only after you meat bags had all run out of power

and keeled over.' Henry extruded a balloon whisk and *zhuzhed* it about in a vaguely menacing manner.

I squatted down and put my arm around Spock. 'Ah.'

'Excellent. I see we're arriving at our destination.' Aurora was hovering at the far side of the bridge.

I stood and turned around to face her. 'Hey, Aurora.' She must have come from Ten Backwards.

'Tickle friend,' cried Spock as she ran to Aurora. She rubbed herself, well, through Aurora's nebulous shape.

'Yeah, we dropped out of warp a few hours ago.' Bexley stood up and turned her back on the view. 'We've been moving under impulse power since then. Our fuel supply just completely conked out when we had the run-in with that other ship. The dilithium crystals, I mean. It was lucky I had … well, that I … you know. Anyways, whatever. We're here now.'

The lift doors opened and BB emerged, Scrappy trailing in her wake. The puppy had opted to stay with BB when I went for a nap while we'd been in warp. I'd been surprised and a bit disappointed but, to be honest, I desperately needed a bit of a break from all the cleaning.

Magenta and pale blue increased in intensity until they were Aurora's dominant colours. 'Well, hello. Who do we have here?'

I scooted over and scooped the puppy up before she could destroy the bridge. 'This is our guest, Scrappy.'

A darker blue joined the other colours in the gaseous cloud that was Aurora. 'Well, yes. I gathered that. But I meant the adult peri with her. Won't someone introduce me?'

I bit my lip, then remembered I was trying not to do that. There was no pain, but BB had warned me not to put any added stress on the repaired flesh. I looked at my shoes instead. Bexley had her head tilted, her golden locks cascading over her shoulder. Henry turned in slow circles on the spot.

Spock ran to BB and nudged her with her long nose. 'Doctor friend.'

BB clucked. 'Aurora, don't you recognise me? It's me, BB, the ship's doctor.'

'Your spouse,' I added. Was I the only one who'd hit my head this morning? Why was everyone acting so weird?

Yellow bloomed throughout Aurora's nebulous shape: embarrassment. 'Oh dear. I'm sorry, love. I'm not sure what's going on in my mind. For a moment, I could've sworn you were someone else. How strange.'

'Maybe I should take you down to the sickbay,' said BB. 'I can, er, check you over before we join the others in the, er...' BB turned to face the rest of us. 'Where are we exactly?'

'Motorway services,' I said.

'It was the only inhabited place we could get to,' said Bexley. 'They're open all day, every day. And even if they don't have what I need to repair the engine, they should be able to order stuff in for fairly quick delivery.'

'Ditto for the parts I'll need to fix the barking comm system,' added Henry.

BB looked at us but stretched one of her upper arms out towards Aurora. 'Why don't you lot head on in to the station? I'll check Aurora over and we'll join you shortly.'

Aurora flashed bright pink for just a second. Weird, I'd always thought that colour meant confusion. Maybe she really wasn't feeling well.

Bexley pranced towards the lift door. 'Okay, cool. The station's tiny. We shouldn't be hard to find. Come on, Lem. Let's go see what they've got for us!' She grabbed my arm and hauled me towards the lift. Scrappy jumped from my arms and ran to BB.

'Oh. You're staying here, are you?'

Scrappy hopped up on her hind legs and pawed at BB to pick her up.

BB scooped the puppy up and turned to me. 'I think you've got your answer there, Lem.'

7 / A FULLY FUNCTIONAL ROBOT

A few minutes later, four of us – Henry, Bexley, Spock, and I – stepped through the docking bay door into Donut Station.

We found ourselves in a sort of parking level beneath the station proper. The curved corridor was brightly lit and relatively clean, but a bit battered. Windows ringed the outer edge of the claustrophobic station. The walls were some sort of greenish stone or plastic, showing scratches and dings. A flashing purple arrow pointed us to the right. We passed two more docking bay doors – both empty – before we got to the lift.

I pressed the button and the door opened immediately, sounding like someone dragging a metal filing cabinet across a cattle grid. There was plenty of space, as lifts go, so we all got in.

When the door creaked open on the station's main level a moment later, we were greeted by … 'Henry?'

'Chunky bunting and goat-blockers!' If Henry had been human, she would definitely have been rolling her eyes and sighing melodramatically. 'It's one of *them*, the absolute curtains.'

'Good morning, afternoon, or evening to you, travellers,' said Henry's doppelgänger. 'Welcome to Donut Station. How may I be of service to you? Is it nutrition you require? Or perhaps assistance with ship repairs?'

The newcomer's voice sounded familiar. *Was that*—? She spoke with a voice that was cheerful and mumsy. Or maybe a primary school teacher. In fact, I wasn't entirely certain her voice didn't belong to one of my teachers.

No.

That's how it worked – Holly assigned a voice to everyone I met. Either it was someone I had known in real life or a voice from telly or podcasts. Spock spoke with my late father's voice. It should have been weird, but it actually made it feel like he was here with me. I like to think he'd be proud of who I became and what I was doing with my life.

The robot extruded a host of different tools and instruments from her blue cylindrical body. Somehow, though, there was something graceful and delicate about her movements. You know, compared to the indignance and menace with which Henry did the same thing.

'We have a selection of parts for the most common brands of ships and assorted equipment, but if what you need isn't in stock, we can order it for you. In most cases, delivery can be arranged in a day or two at most. Please, let me show you to our lounge.' She wheeled away from us, two spatula-like arms beckoning us to follow. 'We have an array of multi-species furniture. The comfort of our guests is our primary—'

'Can it, you obsequious bucket of spare code,' growled Henry. 'Just show us the list of parts you keep in stock.'

The not-Henry person was clearly another member of the same species, the lonely robots. Her voice was plaguing me. I could almost see who it was – but not quite. She paused while Henry spoke but otherwise disregarded her. '—concern. I'll provide you with access to our catalogue of engineering parts and other items for purchase as well as a menu of nutritional goods. If you're looking for sexual companionship, we have an array of holo-programmes. And, of course, though it's not my primary purpose, I should let you know that I am fully—'

'That's enough out of you, muffler ducker. Just show us the pumpkin catalogue and leave us the park alone.'

After pausing to let Henry speak, the other robot continued where she had left off. '—functional, programmed in many—'

'Kryten!' It was. That was Robert Llewellyn's voice.

'Yes, how may I be of assistance to the customer?' Clearly, Holly had taken my exclamation as intent to make that the robot's name. I couldn't fault it for that. It seemed appropriate given her personality – which was all the more jarring for her physical resemblance to Henry.

'You just keep on rolling, you mindless piece of asphalt,' said Henry. 'And yes, I will keep yammering all the way to wherever it is you're pucking taking us, you useless clamp. Bexley here thinks she can talk the hind legs off an equidae – but she's about to see who the real master talker is. One of us doesn't have to stop for a cupping breath every few seconds. Plus, when you factor in my CPU speed, I think you'll find I can keep this up as long as needed.'

I mentally tuned Henry's words out as Kryten led us all to a tall door. One I didn't have to duck through. In a world where most doors were about shoulder-height on me, that was a luxury.

Beyond the door, we arrived in, well, what looked like a fast food restaurant. Or an old-fashioned diner. But with big, comfy-looking booths. Actually, it reminded me of the 'break-out space' at my old office in Canary Wharf. Except with an assortment of species-appropriate furniture. The light next to the door flickered every few seconds.

Henry carried on with her blithering as we took our places at the somewhat bedraggled bar.

'Is…' Every time there was the merest hint of a pause between Henry's words, Kryten tried to get a word – or at least a syllable – in. '…there…'

'…an…'

'…y…'

'…thing…'

After a minute or two, she just gave up and wheeled away. I picked at a worn bit of Formica on the counter.

'Treats?' asked Spock hopefully.

'Not yet, sweetie.' I stared at the departing robot until she was out of earshot. Not that she even had ears. 'Henry, what the hell was that?' I dropped onto a surprisingly comfy stool.

'Holy crap, Henry. What happened to her?' Bexley dragged over a stool suited to her shape and mounted it, her whole body buzzing with pent-up energy.

Henry extruded about a gazillion different implements at once and stirred, turned, vibrated, or shook them all at once. 'I don't want to cladding talk about it.'

'Is she broken? Has her programming been overwritten?' Bexley bounced on her stool. 'Why is she acting like … well, you know … *that*? Do you think she's been enslaved? How else would someone have been able to perform a complete personality wipe?'

'I said we're not going to discuss it.' Henry wheeled in tight circles, nearly running over Spock's paws. 'Sorry.'

'But she might need our help,' Bexley continued. It had only been a few days since we last left Deep Space Five, where our new friends, the kobolds, were only beginning to recover from hundreds of years of generational trauma after being enslaved by the plenties.

'There's nothing technically wrong with that falcon idiot vacuum,' growled Henry. 'Just leave it at that.'

I tugged on my left ear. 'But why is she acting like that? There's got to be a reason for her weird behaviour.'

'She's not trucking defective.' Henry's voice was so low, I barely caught the words.

I sat bolt upright. 'Of course she's defective. Didn't you see how servile she was being? That can't be normal.'

'Just leave it,' Henry said. 'Look at the catalogue or the menu or literally any-plucking-thing else and just drop it, sandwiches.'

'But…' Bexley began. Henry vented a sharply scented gas and then left the diner. If she'd been a teenage human, she would have slammed the door behind herself. But she wasn't and I wasn't even sure how you would go about slamming an automatic sliding door.

Bexley looked at me, her massive horsey jaw hanging slack.

I shrugged. 'I don't know, Bex. I don't understand either. But it's clear she really doesn't want to talk about it.' I pulled my phone out of my pocket and waved it in the air. 'Figure out what you need to buy and place your order. I'll call BB and see if Aurora's feeling any better.'

'Yeah, I guess.' Bexley pulled her phone out of her holster and started clicking and swiping.

'Holly,' I said to my AI. 'Ring BB for me, please.'

'Of course, Lem. Calling her now.' BB didn't answer right away, so I pulled up the station's catalogue on my phone – helpfully translated into English by Holly. As I always tend to do, I scrolled to the food section. I like seeing what other species and cultures eat.

Under 'palatable snacks' it listed an assortment of items, some of which I'd tried elsewhere. A few items had a warning, helpfully added by Holly, that they weren't suited for my biology. But one item caught my eye – mainly because of the flashy advert that was repeated on every single page. 'Pre-made packets of Tasty Bean Paste. Now available in three flavour variants: cotyledon, oleaginous, or bitter.'

'Ew. No thanks. Ooh, they have helbru. I'm going to order a vat of that. Anyone else want anything?' I could definitely do with some caffeine. Well, not caffeine exactly – and certainly not coffee. But it was usually hot and not horrible and it contained a mild stimulant. I mean, not *completely* horrible.

Holly spoke into my ear. 'I'm sorry, Lem. I'm still not getting any answer on BB's line.'

To be honest, I'd forgotten I'd called her. 'Huh, is everything okay?' I continued scrolling through the menu.

'I'm not reading any alerts,' Holly replied. I decided not to read too much into it. She was probably in the middle of something.

I looked at the others. 'Anyone want anything?'

Spock perked her head up at that. 'Delicious treats?'

'Yeah, I'll get you something, mate. Bexley? Hot apple juice?'

Bexley had her nose in her phone, presumably looking up whatever she needed to get us back on the road. 'Yeah, sure. Thanks.'

I stood up, wondering how I was going to find Kryten. But as soon as I stood, she rolled out from behind the counter. 'Hello again, customer. Have you determined your requirements? Is there anything I can help you find?'

Kryten seemed so desperate to please. Bexley was right: it was strange behaviour. 'Um, my friends are still looking at your catalogue to determine what we need for our repairs. But I'd like to order some refreshments while we wait. Is that okay?'

'Absolutely! You are the customer, after all.' Her cheerful voice reminded me of the computer on the *Heart of Gold* in *Hitchhiker's Guide*. If Kryten had eyes, she'd be batting her lashes at me. 'Anything you like, I can provide – within legal limits, obviously. Not that you seem like the sort of customers who might be after anything less than legitimate, of course. I can see you're all completely above board. All your crew, that is. I'm not so sure about your robot – but it's none of my concern.'

'Er, okay.' I opened my mouth to continue, but then closed it. Then tried again. 'So, er… Do you get a lot of the other type out here? People after illegal stuff, I mean.'

'Best not to speak of such things,' Kryten tapped an appendage on her lid. 'Now, what can I get you?'

Interesting.

I ordered drinks for all of us – well, for Bexley, Spock, and me. And decided to take a chance on some fried dough bites I'd spotted on the menu.

'Give treats,' said Spock when I sat back down.

I put my hands on my hips. 'Patience, please. Hen— I mean Kryten will bring them when they're ready. How are you getting on, Bexley? Did you find everything you need to get us moving again?'

Before she could answer, the door to the diner whooshed open again.

Kryten sped across the diner and greeted Aurora and ran through her spiel about being able to provide anything the customer required. Then she led her to our seats – not that it would be easy to miss us without a guide.

'Right this way, please,' Kryten said. 'Your friends have

ordered a selection of refreshments, which I'll bring shortly. If there's anything you'd like to add, please do let me know. My sole purpose is to serve.'

Aurora floated into position next to me, her full rainbow on display. 'Thank you. That will be all for now.'

Kryten rolled through a door behind the counter.

'Hey, Aurora.' Bexley stabbed a hoof in the direction of the closing door. 'She's weird, right? That robot, I mean. Like, not good weird. I mean, you know me. Lord knows I love an oddball. The stranger the better. Like, who even wants to be normal? One of my dads is forever laughing at me and the way I ... well...' She paused and looked at the floor. 'Actually, now that I think about it – that's not good laughter.'

One of her dads had betrayed her in the recent court case, telling the entire galaxy that Bexley was a unicorn and that she deserved to be locked up. Permanently.

I forced my jaw to unclench and put a hand on Bexley's shoulder.

Bexley took a deep breath and then shook her mane out. 'Never mind. But you know what I mean, right? About Kryten? Like, there is something off about her, yeah? Why is she so desperate to please us?'

I nodded but it was Aurora who spoke first. 'Oh, I don't know. She seems perfectly lovely to me.'

I worried at my lip before responding – before considering whether it was still healing. There wasn't any pain, but that could just be the drugs. 'Yeah, sure. She's lovely. But ... I think that's exactly what Bexley means. Why is she so over-the-top perky and servile? She's smarmy. It's ... puzzling, no?'

'Why shouldn't she be?' Aurora was an amalgam of pale and invisible colours.

The door slid aside again. Kryten returned with a tray full of drinks and goodies. She extended several arms and began doling the refreshments out. She placed the bowl of water on the floor for Spock, followed by mugs on the countertop for Bexley and me. I glanced down at the translucent purple liquid and inhaled the floral scent of my helbru.

Kryten waved an implement in the direction of my mug. 'I always add just a drop of dandelion treacle to the helbru. It's the traditional way of serving it on Lazgar Beta. The bitterness offsets the yeasty taste many people complain about in helbru.' Gesturing to Bexley's mug, she added, 'And I put a drop of seaweed in your hot apple juice. It's the latest fad. And I made the donuts this morning. I hope you enjoy your comestibles. Please do let me know if anything's not to your liking. It is my honour to serve. I won't rest until you're all completely satisfied.'

It was utterly bizarre to hear such fawning words come from someone who was physically identical to Henry.

'Right, er... Thank you, Kryten.' I felt like I should say something else. 'Er... How are you?'

A little light on her ... at the top of her ... on the little black band at the top of her cylindrical form, where the body met the lid ... flashed red briefly. 'So long as the customers are satisfied, then I am satisfied.' She bleeped cheerfully then wheeled away.

How did bleeps sound cheerful?

8 / REALLY, REALLY
GOOD DONUTS

I sat back down and took a sip of the helbru. The bright purple liquid normally tasted like Marmite water with a slightly floral aftertaste. But this… 'Oh my gosh! I have no idea what the hell dandelion treacle is, but it makes a world of difference.' On Earth, I'd once had a tisane with chocolate and oat. This tasted like that. But creamier. 'I mean, okay, it's no flat white, but as helbru goes, this is incredible, Kryten. Best I've ever had.'

'Mmm… My apple juice too,' said Bexley. 'I never would have thought of adding seaweed. But it works. It's amazing.'

Spock smacked her lips. 'Peanut butter water.'

Clutching my mug of now-delicious helbru, I looked at Aurora. 'So where are BB and Scrappy? Is everything all right?'

Aurora's colours cast a warm rainbow glow across the diner's floor. 'Hmm, yes. Everything's fine. BB wanted to get some rest. You know what those peri are like, sleeping half their lives away. And I left Scrappy to keep her company.'

'And what about you? Are you feeling any better?' Bexley fidgeted in her seat. 'That was so weird how your memory seemed to, like, glitch out on you? Not recognising your own spouse? That's really bizarre.'

'Oh, I'm fine,' said Aurora. 'Nothing to worry about here.'

'You're sure? You don't need more time to rest as well, do you?' I didn't like to think of her taking unnecessary risks but Aurora had spent several years unable to leave the ship. Now she made the most of every opportunity to explore new places – even unremarkable little service stations in the arse end of nowhere.

'Absolutely,' she replied. 'Thank you. Now, who's buying supplies? I don't know who stocked the *Teapot*'s kitchen last, but it's full of that awful nutrient porridge. Nothing decent to eat.'

Bexley and I exchanged puzzled glances. She stretched a hoof out towards our friend. 'Are you sure you're okay, Aurora?'

Aurora sounded unconcerned. 'Of course. Why wouldn't I be?'

'Well, it's just… You don't eat,' I said.

Bexley pushed her mane over her shoulders. Her long, lustrous golden mane was almost back to the length it was when I first met her. An unfortunate run-in with an unknown substance a few months ago had led to an urgent haircut before the corrosive effects could touch her skin. 'And, you know, you're the one in charge of stocking the ship with domestic supplies. You've always said that the nutrient porridge is the most efficient option. We do bring in fresh fruit and snacks sometimes. And you keep a seemingly unlimited stash of flavourings… But whatever. Are you really, really, *really* sure you're all right?'

Aurora glowed indigo. 'Of course, dear. I'm only concerned about your needs.'

We fell into a mildly awkward silence.

'Oh! I almost forgot. We have donuts.' I reached across the table to grab one of the fried dough bites. Pale green dough. I'd learnt better than to pop new foods straight into my mouth, so I gave it a good sniff first. 'Smells like … wood shavings?'

I broke a tiny piece off and took a small bite. The donut had a beautiful texture: light and fluffy with a hint of chewiness. But it didn't taste of anything at all.

Kryten chose that moment to reappear. 'Try it with the burnt rue dipping sauce. I think you'll like this one.' She waved a pointy tool at one of several ramekins, which contained what appeared to be a pale blue chutney of some sort.

I spooned a tiny drop of the sticky blue substance onto my donut and touched it tentatively to my tongue.

'Oh my gosh!' The dipping sauce completely changed the experience. I dunked the whole donut in and shoved it into my mouth. 'Zhish izh abayzhug.' The chutney, or whatever it was, tasted of lemony caramel. That sounds like it shouldn't work but, trust me, it did.

Bexley frowned. 'What?'

'Give Spock.' Spock was leaving an ocean of drool on my shoes. 'Give tasty donut.'

Kryten indicated another ramekin with one appendage. 'The equidae customer may like this one. It's firegrass jam.' She motioned towards a third dish. 'And your quadruped friend may enjoy this starflower seed hummus.'

I forced myself to swallow the mouthful. 'Sorry, it's amazing. Light and delicious – just the right amount of sweetness. Sort of citrusy. It basically melted on my tongue. It's like heaven in a tiny ball of heaven.'

Spock rose up off her bum then sat back down, her tail

swishing madly. 'Give Spock.' She slapped my arm with her paw.

I dipped one in the pink hummus and handed it to her – which she swallowed without even tasting. 'More.' She stood on her hind legs and tried to grab the plate off the table.

'No,' I barked, shoving the plate firmly out of her reach – definitely because I wasn't impressed with her lack of manners and not anything to do with me not wanting to share. Almost certainly. 'How are you getting on with your shopping, Bexley?'

'Just … about … there.' She clicked a few buttons on her phone before looking up at me. 'There we go. I've placed my order for the unobtainium. According to the app, it's got a twenty-one-hour turnaround. All we have to do now is wait. I should go check with Henry … see how she's getting on with the ansible parts she needs.'

She picked up a donut and dipped it into the firegrass jam. She was halfway across the diner when she turned around. 'Oh my gosh. This is fantastic. Spicy and bitter – I love it. Thanks for that dip, Kryten. That's really considerate of you.'

'It is always my pleasure to provide customers with a positive experience,' said Kryten before returning to the kitchen.

I leant back in my seat and scrolled through the station's catalogue. In addition to fuel and parts and the café, they also offered an extensive supermarket section. Curious, I looked through what was available. Most of the listings didn't mean much of anything to me, though a few seemed familiar. Dihydrogen monoxide. Stearic acid. Crystallised disaccharides. Sodium hydrogen carbonate. Pulverised Triticum aestivum seeds. Phenolic aldehyde.

Hang on. Disaccharides? Wasn't that sugar?

On a whim, I ordered five kilograms of all those things.

'So.' I popped yet another little donut into my mouth. 'Now I guess we just wait.'

Aurora didn't say anything. Spock farted softly in her sleep.

'I suppose… Should we go see what Bexley's up to? Maybe explore the station a bit?' Spock thumped her tail on the floor a few times before jumping up. I waited a few moments for Aurora to respond. When she didn't say anything, I waved at her. 'Aurora?'

'Hmm?'

I jabbed a thumb back towards the diner's entrance. 'Are you coming with me?'

'No, dear. You go ahead. I'm going to stay here and order some food.'

'What?' Rubbing a hand along the back of my neck, I took a step backwards. When I realised she must have meant stocking up supplies for the ship, I waved my question away. 'Never mind. All right. I'll see you in a bit then. Spock, I assume you're coming with me?'

'Spock protect.'

I stroked her ears. 'Pretty sure I'll be safe on this little station, mate. But I suppose you can keep any eye out for any attack donuts, eh?'

'Tasty donuts.'

Chuckling, I waved at Aurora.

On my way to the door back to the concourse, I looked around – just a large room filled with tables and booths. Some bigger, some smaller, and clearly designed for a host of different physiologies – but all with a relatively consistent design. The whole place was clean, but it all looked a bit worse for the wear. The light next to the door still flickered.

We headed back out the way we'd entered. I touched a finger to the broken light next to the door.

As I passed the lift, I spotted Bexley and Henry stood next to a viewing port. They were talking to… I'm not quite sure how to describe her. She appeared to be entirely made of arms. Imagine dozens of arms all joined at the elbow – making a sort of peachy-beige-brown Christmas tree of weirdness.

'Hey, Lem! Lem! Lem! Come over here. You've got to hear this. I mean, unless you're not you. But how do we know if you're not you?' She turned to face the tree-arm person – Treena, for want of a better name. 'Oh gosh. How do we know Lem's not the one you're looking for? I mean, I know it's not me. Though I suppose it could be Henry.'

'Guac you,' said Henry.

Bexley spun to face Henry, her mane swishing gracefully as she moved. 'Okay, probably not you, to be fair. But it could be Lem. Or Spock. Or anyone, really. Do you have a plan?' She spun back to face Treena, who hadn't actually said a word yet. Could a tree-arm person even speak?

'It could be any of you.' Treena's various arms swayed slightly as she spoke. 'I know it's not me – I've been hunting the creature for months.'

I pinched the bridge of my nose. 'Could someone please tell me what is going on? Who could be whom?'

Treena backed away from me. 'The shifter. It could be you. Or you. Or you. Or even you.' One finger on each of four arms pointed at Henry, Bexley, Spock, and 'even' me.

Spock licked the hand Treena was pointing at her.

'The shifter? What shifter? What are you talking about?' My feet shuffled of their own accord. 'What even is a shifter?'

'You would say that, wouldn't you?' muttered Treena. 'Of course you'd say that.'

'Our entirely rational friend here says she's been hunting a carping changeling.' Henry wheeled herself a bit further from Treena. 'She says the creature lays barking traps for unsuspecting ships. Traps that not only drain a ship's vexing dilithium crystals, but also knock out their pumpkin ansibles.'

Bile rose in my throat. 'What?'

Bexley was tap-dancing on the spot. 'And then, when the ship sends a team in to investigate, the changeling secretly poses as one of their crew members. You know, because they can shapeshift. Like, I don't mean they just impersonate them, they actually, physically *transform* into them. Isn't that amazing?'

Treena raised one of her gazillion hands in something like a stop gesture. 'Or sometimes they may pose as innocent victims of the same trap.'

Bexley tapped her hooves in the air. 'Yeah, so like, one member of the crew isn't who they say they are anymore. And now they're acting to get rid of the actual crew.'

My eyes went wide as I felt the blood drain from my face. 'Get rid?'

'The victims are sometimes dumped on an unsuspecting space station,' added Treena. 'Occasionally, they've even been pushed out the airlock.'

'What?' I forced myself to swallow down my fear.

'Your precious little Scrappy isn't who she frocking says she is,' growled Henry. 'She's not an innocent baby. She's a shapeshifting criminal.'

'Or, well, like, probably half of one,' added Bexley.

'What?' Since leaving Earth, far too many of my contributions to conversations amounted to that single, unhelpful syllable. Though, now that I thought about it, my contributions on Earth may not have been much better.

'Scrappy.' Henry paused. 'Is not.' She paused again. 'An inn—'

I swatted her words away with a flick of my wrist. 'Yeah, I heard you the first time. I'm just having trouble processing what you're telling me. How can she be this … this … changeling? Are they even real?'

Bexley bumped her hooves together several times in quick succession. 'Oh, I watched this really interesting documentary one time about how shifter molecular biology works, actually. It's totally fascinating the way … they can … no. Hang on. I think that might have been porn. Maybe one of those erotic game shows. Whatever. Never mind.'

I glanced at her out the corner of my eye then looked from Henry to Treena and back again. 'So … they are real?'

'Clerking real,' said Henry.

'Definitely real.' Treena was wringing at least four of her hands.

'So...' I wasn't sure where to go with that statement or question or whatever. Remember what I was saying about my valuable contributions?

'So ... we need to figure out who's the shifter,' said Bexley.

A thought occurred to me. 'Shouldn't Spock be able to sniff them out? Presumably a changeling wouldn't smell the same as the person she's posing as, right? Actually, wait. Bexley, isn't your sense of smell as st—'

Treena raised one of her arms, index finger extended. 'Aha, what an interesting observation. Quite wrong, of course, but interesting nonetheless. You see, when a shifter takes a new form, it's not copying merely the person's outward appearance, but rather becoming them on a molecular level. A cursory DNA test wouldn't reveal the difference. Though, obviously the full genome sequence would reveal any number of anomalies.'

She waggled a few of her hands around expressively. 'As would any detailed scan. For example, the creature is bound by physical laws, such as conservation of mass. So, while its mimicries will comprise the correct types of molecules, it will contain the wrong number of them. Through this means, it can transform into something much larger or smaller than itself ... though its mass will always remain the same. And it can divide itself—'

'Huh?' Another stunningly valuable contribution. 'So there's literally no way at all to distinguish between the real person and the fake – at least until they shift—'

Henry extruded a spongy ball on the end of a long, articulated arm and bopped me on the forehead with it. 'She literally just said the genome sequence or a detailed physical scan, you lump of under-proved dough.'

'Ow, you jerk.' I waved her weapon away. 'Do you happen to have copies of all our genome sequences or detailed scans? Because unless you do, we still don't have any way of distinguishing the real person from the … the … creature, shifter, thing.'

Treena waggled a finger at me. 'Aha, but the monster is only a *physical* copy.'

'Okay.' Wait – did she say monster?

'Ooh, oh, oh! I think I get you, Treena,' said Bexley. 'A person's soul, her katra, the essence of what makes her *her* … isn't physical, right? So, like, the shifter can copy a person's physical presence, but she can't actually *be* the person she's impersonating, right? Like, that's not a thing that's within her power, is it? Oh! Unless she's also psychic. She's not psychic, is she?'

Treena shuffled sideways on several of her hands. 'No, it cannot read a person's mind. In fact, usually she can't pass even a basic inspection. And let's be clear – we are not talking about a fully fledged sapient. It's merely an animal. A skilled mimic – but nonetheless, an animal acting on pure base instinct.'

'Right,' said Henry. 'In that case, we just have to ask everyone a few basic questions to test their knowledge and see if their personality matches what we expect. Works for everyone except the furless bear here – she has no personality to test against.'

'Hey,' I said … but then couldn't figure out where to go with my objection.

'Actually,' said Treena. 'I've developed a test. I have a device that creates a sonic field that briefly interrupts the shifter's grasp on the form it's holding. As a result, it reverts to its natural form for a few seconds.'

'Does it hurt?' I asked.

'Oh, yes,' said Treena. 'Immensely.' She sounded *immensely* proud of this fact. 'But only when used on a changeling.'

'Why – are you worried you might be the goatherding creature?'

I scowled. 'No, Henry. I'm worried we might be inflicting pain on innocent people.'

Bexley tapped her hooves in the air. 'And, for that matter, I suppose that the creature – assuming Treena's right that it's an *it* and not a *she* – is only acting to protect itself and isn't actually intending to harm anyone. So, while I agree we need to stop it, we should do so without harming the creature.'

Treena clenched several fists. 'Of course, of course.'

'So, er...' I closed my eyes for a moment to gather my thoughts. 'If the creature ... the shifter or changeling or whatever ... is really just a sort of mindless animal, then what does it want? Why is it replacing people?'

Bexley spun to face Treena. 'Yeah, Lem's got a point? What's its goal?'

'In my experience —' began Treena.

But Henry cut her off. 'What *is* your sharding experience, anyway?'

If Treena had lips, she definitely would have pursed them then. 'As it happens, I am a xenobiologist. I completed my doctorate in the differences and commonalities between ethnoshifter communities and pre-sapient changelings. I have studied two mature sapient species, one immature sapient species, and no less than four non-sapient species across the alpha, gamma, and delta quadrants. I have written a dozen papers for pre —'

'All right, all right, we get it,' said Henry. 'Cup. No one wants to hear your entire CV, arm-y.'

Treena raised a hand to clutch at her – er – one of her other arms. 'I'll have you know I've tracked this creature across twelve parsecs. I've visited these creatures in their home sector and studied them in their natural habitat. I've been on this one's tail since it got loose from the Calivon.'

'Fine,' growled Henry. 'Now what? Do you have this testing device on you?'

Treena shuffled even further away from Henry. 'The device is in my ship. I propose we all go together to get it.'

'Why?' I caught myself starting to worry at my bottom lip and took a slow breath instead. 'That is, er… It's not that we don't trust you. It's just… Well, we don't all have to go, do we? Why don't we go wait in the diner with Aurora?' I jabbed a thumb in the direction of the station's café.

'I would have thought it was obvious.' Treena waved several of her hands. 'We don't know who the beast is. It's likely someone on this station has already been replaced. But who? We should all stay together until we can capture it and deliver it to the shifter sanctuary on Talos.'

I scratched my ear. 'Until we get the testing device, you mean, right?'

Henry poked at me with an arm that looked like a shower scrubby. 'You really are a stupid effigy, cactus. If any of us take our eyes off one another, we can't be certain that the changeling doesn't replace one of us.'

'Oh.' I hadn't considered that.

'Right, well, I guess you'd better lead us to your ship then, Treena,' said Bexley. 'And maybe while we walk, you can tell us how you ended up here.'

Treena moved towards the lift, walking on some of her hands. 'Yes, well, as I said, I've tracked the creature across twelve parsecs. But I lost it a few days ago – along with my ship. It did as it always does – killed my engine and my comms devices – so I knew it couldn't have gone far. But I escaped in the life pod and came here. It took me six days to traverse the distance.'

The lift door creaked open as we approached.

'Oh, wow,' said Bexley as we all moved into the lift. 'It's lucky that happened close enough to anywhere that could save you.'

'Yeah, lucky,' replied Henry. 'Forgive me if I sound some- what cynical.'

'It's only because you're a cynic,' I added.

The lift door groaned open on the parking level and we followed Treena out and to the right. If I had to guess, I figured there were berths for about six ships, though only a couple were visible at any given time.

Floor-to-ceiling windows lined the deck, broken only by a

series of docking bay doors. The *Teapot* gleamed fuchsia. A few bays along, we discovered a small grey ship. It looked like a minivan. A really boxy minivan. No wonder we hadn't spotted it before. Well, that and the fact it was on the opposite side of the station from the *Teapot*.

I pressed my face to the window. 'It's not much bigger than a transporter pod.'

Treena pressed her hand to the reader next to the door, before pulling the door aside. 'Well, yes. I did say it was an escape pod.'

Henry, Bexley, Spock, and I crowded around the door. Beyond it, the ship's single room was visible. It wasn't any bigger on the inside.

Treena opened a drawer and removed a device that looked like, well, like a sort of sonic screwdriver. 'Aha, yes. Here we go. I'll test myself first, shall I?'

'Yeah, you do that,' said Henry.

Treena used one hand to point the device at herself and another to activate it. It glowed green and emitted a soft whirring sound. 'See? No pain. Just a slight tickle.'

Popty ping, said the device. 'Not a shifter,' Treena announced.

Treena repeated the process with Henry and then Bexley. When it was Spock's turn, she shook her head the way she did when I tickled her ears.

Finally, Treena pointed the device at me. I felt a small vibration of the air.

The device popped and pinged once again. 'Not a shifter,' Treena announced for the fifth time.

Bexley raised her hooves. 'There we go. None of us is the creature. So now we just need to check everyone else.'

Since we were already on Donut Station's docking bay

level, we decided to do a quick search of the *Teapot*. Well, as quick as possible. The *Teapot* was of a similar size to the station – possibly even a bit bigger.

Henry rolled up to the door where our ship was docked. She extruded a hinged metal arm and entered the code to unlock the door.

As I followed the others in something struck me. 'You know how strangely Aurora was behaving earlier, right?'

We all stepped in. 'She was,' Henry said before instructing the lift to take us to the top deck.

'You don't think—' began Bexley but Treena cut her off.

'If you observed behaviour that was markedly different from your friend's normal, it could indicate—'

Bexley's nostrils flared. 'I can't believe none of us noticed that something was wrong. I mean, okay, so the notion she's been replaced by a malicious changeling wasn't exactly an obvious conclusion for us to reach. You know, considering most of us have never even met one. But you know what I mean, right? Like we should have picked up on the fact that *something* was off. Shouldn't we? I mean, she didn't recognise her own spouse.'

As the lift door slid open, we stepped out onto the bridge. From this angle, the *Teapot*'s clear dome showed a whole lot of stars … and not much else.

I stopped walking and turned to face her. 'We did notice. And we all thought she wasn't feeling well. Everything's happened so quickly today. We all saw she was acting a bit strangely and we did the most logical thing – we asked BB to check her out. I don't see what else we could have done.'

We followed Henry and Treena into the lounge – the room where all this had started, at least for me. No sign of BB or Scrappy.

'Hey, so, er… If this creature has posed as Aurora, what's happened to the real Aurora?'

Both Henry and Bexley stopped moving. Bexley looked at me, then at Treena.

'That's…' Henry wheeled in a tight circle. 'That's a surprisingly astute question coming from the animatronic dildo over there.'

Treena stretched out an arm towards me. 'Ah, yes. It's quite interesting, actually. I've observed the usurpation patterns of no less than four different shifter species. They all have their own unique behaviours – rituals one might call them in the higher species.'

'Spare us the lecture, hand-y.' Henry jabbed Treena with an implement that looked like a tuning fork. 'Just tell us what happened to our friend.'

I'd never heard Henry call anyone *friend* before. She had to be freaking out.

Treena waved several of her hands. 'Oh, don't worry. She'll probably be fine. Hopefully. Assuming we find her in time. The beast isn't malevolent. It just incapacitates its victims.'

'If the plucker's left her on board, we'll find her.' Henry rolled towards the ship's centre column. 'Let's check the loo and then we can move onto the next floor.'

We all peered into the toilet cubicle. The sink, walls, and mirror were all still spattered in my blood from when I'd injured myself early this morning.

Treena raised several of her hands in alarm – or, well, in something that looked like alarm to me. 'Someone's been attacked.'

I shook my head. 'Oh, that. No, nothing like that. When the ship dropped out of warp, I fell and hit my head.' I gestured at my missing teeth. 'Injured myself. Cut my lip. Broke my nose.'

Thanks to hanging around Henry, I'd grown used to being glared at by people without eyes. I could feel Treena looking at me funny. 'You must be very clumsy.'

I kind of bobbled my head. Not quite a nod – but not *not* a nod either.

Once we'd completed a reasonably thorough search of the *Teapot*, we headed back to the station. But as we stepped out onto the floor of the parking level, something didn't feel right. I couldn't put my finger on what it was. Judging by their visibly tensed muscles, Bexley and Spock could sense it too.

'Ficus.' Henry wheeled in a tight circle. 'The bollarding exterior lights are out.'

'Oh, yeah.' I looked out the closest window. 'Weren't there lights around the windows before?'

'What the puck do you think I was referring to there, sandwich?' Henry extended a long arm – at least two metres – to her right. 'And over there, the sign advertising the finest donuts this side of Raxacoricofallapatorius. That was lit up before too.'

I shivered. 'To be fair, they're *really* good.'

Bexley tapped her hooves in the air. 'I know, right? There was a planet we used to go to sometimes when I was a kid. They had these sour-spicy fried donuts made from a type of local grass. They're the only ones I've ever had in my life that might be on par with the ones Kryten made —'

'Do you two mind? In case you've forgotten, we've kind of got a plucky shifter to catch.' Henry moved in the direction of the station's central lift. 'And it's already taken one of our friends.'

'Or two,' I said. 'We've not seen BB in a while, either.'

'True.' Bexley tapped her hooves in the air.

Treena scurried after Henry on several of her hands. 'Henry's right. There's definitely something amiss here. If I'm not mistaken, the temperature has dropped a couple of degrees since we left.'

Bexley, Spock, and I caught up with them just as Henry pressed the button to call the lift. 'Three point one four one five degrees, actually.'

The lift doors screeched open and we all rushed in. A moment later, the metal-grinding-on-metal sound made my muscles clench and we emerged on the retail level. Only, instead of Kryten with her servile prattle, there was silence. Half the lights in the place were off. Harsh overhead lights were on, but the lights around the advertising images on the walls were all off. It felt like seeing a pub after hours – when the big lights are all on and you see all the grime. Everything felt cold and institutional rather than warm and welcoming.

When we got to the diner, we found the tables broken and the chairs tossed aside. The screens on the wall were mostly smashed. A few were lying on the floor.

Kryten rolled across the room towards us slowly but purposefully. 'You brought this on us. You've unleashed chaos on this station.' She waved a blue rolling pin at us in a vaguely threatening fashion. 'I hope you've got deep pockets or good insurance. Because you're going to be paying for all this damage.'

It was like she'd had a complete personality transfer. Now

she sounded like the robot in *Hitchhiker's Guide* – specifically, the Alan Rickman version. Bored but also hostile.

Bexley raised her hooves. 'If we've caused any damage, we'll totally pay for it. Of course we will. We're good citizens. But this isn't our fault. I assume the damage was caused by the shifter. And we didn't bring it here.' She brushed her blond mane back over her shoulders. 'I mean, okay, yes. We *did* bring it here. But only literally. We're victims, same as you are. Anyways, what's happened? What's going on?'

Kryten wielded the rolling pin as a truncheon, stabbing it at Bexley. 'As if you don't know.'

Both Henry and Spock moved between Kryten and Bexley, defending our friend.

'Hey, you useless waste of a CPU,' said Henry. 'We flew into that thing's trap. It knocked out our warp drive and our ansible. We were lucky to make it this far so we could order parts to fix our ship.'

'And now it's done the same to us,' replied Kryten – who had apparently decided Henry existed after all. 'Our computer system is down. Our life support is barely functional. And nothing else works at all. Our next re-stocking mission isn't due for more than seventy-seven hours.'

I swallowed. 'Okay, so to prevent anyone else being hurt, we just have to stick together for that long.'

'Hang on.' Bexley stepped towards Kryten. 'I placed a rush on my order so it would be delivered in' – she checked her watch – 'nineteen hours. Why are you saying seventy-seven?'

'If your order went through before the comms went down, they'll be here within the SLA. Otherwise, our default order isn't due for seventy-seven hours.' She sounded like this was all just a plot to inconvenience her. She reversed course, backing away from us. 'And anyway, why on Trantor would I want to stay close to you lot? No chance.'

Bexley held her hooves up in front of herself. 'The thing is we don't know who the beast is. Who it's posing as, I mean. We think it may have been our friend, Aurora. We left her here when we went, well, um… That is, when we went to search our ship. But we haven't seen her since then, so we don't know who the shifter is now. And so we need to keep an eye on each other at all times. But, oh, actually…' She turned to Treena. 'You should check Kryten. You know, with your thingy. In case she's the shifter.'

Kryten extruded a stabby-looking implement and waved it at us. 'I do not consent to any invasive tests.'

'It's not invasive,' I said. 'It's just a little tool that vibrates at a certain frequency.'

On the other side of Kryten, Treena waved her sonic screwdriver. Before Kryten could object further, it popped and pinged.

'She's clear,' said Treena. 'Not a shifter.'

'Of course I'm not a shifter.' Kryten wheeled in big loopy circles. 'If I were, would I really be the one complaining about all the damage she's done?'

Treena lowered her device. 'It.'

Kryten's resemblance to Henry ratcheted up by a mile when she extruded three arms and waved them. 'What?'

Spock walked into the loo.

Treena pointed at her in an agitated fashion. 'Stop! Someone stop her. We can't let anyone out of our sight.'

With a grumble, I followed Spock into the loo. 'Right, why don't we check it's clear? Then we can let Spock do her business in peace while we stand guard over the door. Fair?'

Spock, of course, didn't care who watched her pee. As soon as we all crowded into the small space, she squatted over the hole in the floor. Toilet training her on the *Teapot* had been a snap once we had translators – not to mention toilets she could use.

Treena leapt back out of the splash zone. 'Hey! A little warning wouldn't go amiss.'

Henry sprayed a puff of scented air freshener. 'What? Like you gave me before zapping me with your test?'

Oh, I guess that must have been Kryten, not Henry. Having two identical people really wasn't helping matters.

Bexley ran a hoof down her long nose, pushing her forelock over the stub of her horn. 'Um, if Spock's done now, maybe we can all head back out to the concourse. You know, where there's more room.'

I nodded. 'Good idea.'

Treena crowded behind us as we left the room and the others followed.

Bexley put her hooves on her hips and spun around. 'Well, now what?'

'We still haven't checked Aurora.' I wasn't sure why I was whispering.

'Where is the gas bag?' I was pretty sure that was Henry. At least, I *thought* it was Henry. Since Kryten's apparent personality transplant, I was finding it hard to tell the two robots apart.

Actually… 'Er, Treena. Could you scan everyone again, please?'

Bexley cocked her head to the side. 'They're right – we really do need to find Aurora. Like, if we're right and Scrappy and BB are two halves of this beast, then they could have taken her. Or hurt her. Or become her. We need to find her. The real Aurora.'

'I'm with her.' Henry jabbed a weird sort of thumb in Bexley's direction, then turned it to point at her doppelgänger. 'Since you clearly know your way around this place, you should lead the search.'

Kryten jabbed a feather duster at Henry. 'I'm not leading you people anywhere. Not until you tell me what's going on. What's the beast you keep talking about?'

'Right.' Bexley sort of danced in place. 'You were the one who accused us of releasing some sort of creature on the station – something that's been messing with the electrics and the comms and generally messing the place up. You remember that, right? It was only a few minutes ago.'

'Of course I remember,' said Kryten – her voice dripping with scorn. 'But I was referring to the oaf. I assumed it was she who had done all that.'

'What oaf?' But they were all staring at me. I pulled a face as I shook my head. 'Ugh. It wasn't me. I didn't do all this. For starters, I wouldn't even know how to take out the station's comms system.'

'I can vouch for the corking oaf.'

'Thank you, Henry.' I wasn't accustomed to having her come to my defence.

'Lem's an idiot,' she continued. 'She might've wrecked the booths – but the damage to your comms and electrics is too targeted. She hasn't got the CPU for it.'

Of course. Should've figured that. 'When would I have wrecked the furniture? For that matter, *why* would I have done so—'

Bexley waved my words away. 'There's a changeling on the loose. It's not a person – just a beast. Treena's tracked it across twelve parsecs. She knows all about them. Did her thesis on their mating habits and everything.'

I'm not sure how Kryten – a featureless cylinder – managed it, but she looked sceptical. 'And you think a mind-less beast overrode Donut Station's complex comms array and the specific part of our electrical grid that proclaims to travellers that we're open for business?'

Treena waved multiple hands – probably at least six. 'It's not doing so in any kind of rational way. Rather, it seeks out the electrical signals passing through the cables and destroys them. It's purely an instinctive action – not a rational one.'

'Right.' Kryten pointed something that looked like an ordinary ballpoint pen at Henry. 'Are you buying this?'

'We have to hurry,' shrieked Treena.

Bexley pulled over a small ottoman that had been tossed aside and sat down on it. 'Why though? What's the rush?'

Treena shuffled across the floor and positioned herself directly in front of Bexley. 'It's about to bud!'

My hand shot up to my ear, instinctively trying to protect myself from Treena's too-loud voice. 'Bud?'

Bexley's body language mirrored my own. 'Bud?'

Henry and Kryten both extruded little brushes and waved them around. 'Bud?'

Spock let out a little fart and thumped her tail on the floor.

Treena folded multiple arms across … well, across more arms. 'Bud! Procreate. Reproduce. Make more of itself.'

'Oh,' we all replied in unison.

We looked at one another for a moment. Eventually, Henry flapped a hair clip at Treena. 'How do you know?'

Treena shuffled backwards. 'I beg your pardon?'

'How…' Henry jabbed the hair clip again. 'Do…' Another stab. 'You…'

Treena made multiple flicking motions. 'I am an expert in—'

Henry retracted the clip. 'Yeah, yeah. We've listened to you recite your CV already. My point is … enlighten us.

What is it about the creature's biology or behaviour that's led you to this disturbing conclusion?'

Treena raised about seventeen index fingers. 'That's an excellent question, my robot fr—'

'I'm not your foetid friend. Just answer the fisted question.'

'Of course, of course.' Treena took several steps away from Henry. 'It's a behavioural change. The chaos caused by the creature increases as it tries to build a nest for its offspring in the hours before the budding process begins.'

Bexley pushed her mane back over her shoulders. 'So, um… What exactly does that mean in practice for this species? What are we talking here? A station full of eggs? Does it split into two? Oh, is there going to be a whole litter of little baby shifters? Actually, that brings up another set of questions? Are they born – or hatched, I suppose – or budded – whatever… How long until they're full-blown shifters in their own right?'

I pursed my lips. 'And how many of them are we talking about?'

Treena scuttled away from Bexley – but Kryten spoke first. 'Perhaps we could save the exobiology lesson for a time when there isn't some sort of hellspawn about to burst in this station? I thought we needed to search for your friend who may or may not be your friend?'

I slapped my forehead. 'And BB too!'

Bexley leapt up off her seat and moved to follow Kryten. 'Oh yeah. We should do that.' She turned back. 'Treena, maybe you can tell us about the shifter while we look for BB and Aurora?'

'I can do that.'

'Ugh, fine. Whatever.' Kryten led us across the concourse, through the maze of the wrecked furniture.

As we moved, Henry and Kryten hefted cushions, fallen wall panels, and furniture, shifting them out of our way. But also inspecting them, before tossing them aside.

Bexley stood up and brushed the dust from her legs after peering underneath a mound of debris. 'What's the point of all this damage? What's it trying to achieve?'

Treena scurried out of the way of a cushion Henry – no, Kryten – had sent flying. 'It's nesting. I'm sure I mentioned that already.'

I dropped to my knees to get a good look inside the next mound of detritus. 'And the electrical damage? What's that got to do with its reproductive processes?'

Bexley put her hands on her hips as she looked around. 'Hang on. Is that it? Is this where we started? Have we completed a circuit of the entire concourse? Every part of this deck looks the same as every other part – I can't tell.'

Kryten led a path to a door in the centre of the station. 'We've searched the public areas on this level. I suggest we try the staff-only areas before moving on to the lower level.'

We followed Kryten through a security door into the station's kitchen. No one was visible in the main room – but my eye was drawn to movement off to one side. A big glass door leading to a walk-in fridge or maybe freezer – and inside there was a sparkly rainbow-coloured whirlwind of chaos.

I ran to Aurora, my mind instantly flashing to our first meeting. She'd been hiding in a freezer then, too.

From behind me, Bexley shrieked. When I turned to see why, time seemed to slow down.

Treena was racing across the kitchen. No, that wasn't accurate. She was *stretching* across the room. Her arms elongated, distorting and twisting as she moved. My head snapped back to the walk-in freezer when the door clicked. Aurora seemed to pulsate and solidify as she moved.

No, not *she*, I realised. This wasn't Aurora – it was the beast. Was Treena supposed to be such a contortionist? Or was she also the beast? Had it already budded?

Spock yelped and bolted from the space, just like she'd done when she first met Scrappy. I ran after her – I wouldn't let her be taken. By the time I emerged from the diner, she was clear across the donut-shaped concourse.

I'm not the most graceful, and usually not the most speedy, but I flew across the space as fast as my little legs would carry me, stubbing most of my toes and bashing my shins and swearing a blue streak as I ran.

'Keep Spock in sight. Don't let her be taken,' I instructed

myself in between curses. 'Don't let her be taken over.' I managed to stay upright. Somehow.

The horrendous noise of the lift doors creaking open reached me before I got there. I spun around the corner to the lift, catching up with Spock just before the door closed. Kryten was with her. She must have run in the other direction on the concourse to beat us here.

'Quick, customers' said Kryten. 'Get in.'

I followed Spock into the lift as the door stuttered and then groaned shut.

Collapsing to the floor of the lift, I struggled to catch my breath – more from fright than the short sprint. Probably. Whatever. 'What...? How...? When...? Why...?' I couldn't figure out what I was actually trying to ask, so I leant back against the wall. 'Deep cleansing breaths.' I did a few, counting primes as I went.

But then the wall behind me slid open. I hadn't even noticed there was a second door on the opposite side of the lift.

Kryten held up a lavender triangle and addressed Spock, her perky, mumsy voice firmly back in place. 'Now, technically, guests are not permitted in the station's storeroom areas – but I deduce that your safety is at risk. As such, I'm overriding normal protocols.' The card changed to orange. 'Please, follow me.'

Spock and I followed her into the station's core, into a room lined with rows of crowded shelves. We passed a big bin of those Tasty Bean Paste packets I'd seen on the menu. They looked exactly like they had in the menu image – similar to the little ketchup packets you'd get in an Earth takeaway.

I reached out to one of the shelves and touched a stack of packages. 'Pulverised Triticum aestivum seeds,' announced

Holly. A thought struck me, but I didn't have time to process it.

'If you would be so kind as to complete the questions you asked a moment ago,' said Kryten. 'I'd be delighted to try to answer them. Though, unfortunately, at this point, I'm not sure I'm in possession of any satisfactory replies.'

Drumming my index finger on the package in front of me, I tried to concentrate. 'What?'

'Yes, that was one of them.' She paused and extended a long, jointed appendage around a corner. After a moment, she used the same arm to beckon me to follow. 'Along with "How?", "When?", and "Why?".'

I stopped moving for a moment and studied her. 'Oh, right. Sorry, I mean, I guess we found the beast. Or maybe beasts, plural? I thought they had to abide by conservation of mass. Is the offspring born as big as the parent? And what happened with Treena? Was that normal? Surely one shifter can't become two full-size beings?'

A pale yellow light I'd not previously noticed along Kryten's lid-line lit up and moved around her in a clockwise direction. 'That would seem to be logical.'

Was Kryten not with us when Treena explained about conservation of mass? I couldn't remember.

'But then,' she added, 'we can't judge a being's mass by looking at their physical form.'

A door slid aside, revealing a small, dimly lit room. Along one wall, there was a desk or worktop and the opposite side held a worn but comfy-looking sofa. At the far side of the room, there were four doors. 'This is the staff accommodation section – it doesn't get much use at present. The station owner stays here when she's onboard, but that's only a small portion of the time. The furnishings are sadly basic, but I hope you find it comfortable until the danger is past. I will do my utmost to see to your needs and desires in the interim. The comfort of guests is my primary purpose.'

Kryten rolled towards the far side of the room. 'I'll just verify that the rooms are empty.' The first door she opened was a small bathroom. The next three were rooms just large enough to hold a single bed and not much else. One of the rooms had a pair of shoes – or at least they looked like shoes to me. Another had the bed folded up against the wall, making for a bit more floor space. But they were otherwise unremarkable.

'There you go,' said Kryten. 'You'll be safe here.'

'Find Bexley.' Spock turned to the door's exit. 'Bexley friend.'

I was in the process of sitting down on the sofa – but at Spock's words I stood back up again. 'Yeah. We need to save Bexley. And Henry. And the others.'

Kryten forced her way between Spock and the door, blocking any exit from the room. 'Now that you are safe here, I'll go and seek out Bexley and the others from your crew. Of course, if your robot is lost, you should be able to obtain a replacement easily enough.'

I stabbed my fists into my sides. 'We don't want another robot. Henry is our friend. We want *her*.'

'Spock good girl. Do security.'

'We're going to find our friends.' I made to move past Kryten, then thought better of it. 'But, actually, we all need to stay together. We got split up by mistake, but we should find the others and stick together until a supply ship arrives to rescue us.'

Kryten's lighty-uppy thing flashed purple. 'That would be … unwise. The guests would be safer to remain here.'

'But you don't know who the shifter is.' I sat back down

on the bed. '*Are*. Who the shifters are. We don't even know for sure how many there are. You could lead them right here.'

'I will secure the door and then go seek your friends and bring them back here,' Kryten said, her voice as cheerily obsequious as when we'd first met. The hostility she'd shown on the diner's floor had disappeared entirely.

I threw my hands in the air. 'Or you could be replaced and then come back here to harm us. I'm telling you – we *need* to stay together. We can't let anyone out of our sight.'

'As you wish.' Kryten gestured through the open door. 'Where would you suggest we start our search?'

'Bexley.' Spock headed off in the direction we'd just come.

I shrugged. 'Follow her nose, I guess.'

Spock led us back towards the lift – but then zigged when I thought she was going to zag. She sniffed the air.

'Er, Spock.' I pointed at the lift door. 'Shouldn't we head back up to the kitchen?'

'Doctor friend.' She headed through a smaller door – into the parking level.

'No, Spock,' I whispered. 'She's—' But as I came around the bend, BB was right in front of me.

BB lifted her wings in greeting. 'Oh, there you are. Thank heavens I found you. You'll never believe what happened.' Behind her, the row of windows showed the *Teapot* docked in the same spot it had been earlier.

The muscles in my jaw clenched involuntarily as I backed away from her. She could be the changeling. But then, I had to keep her sweet in case she really was. 'Oh, hey, BB. What? What happened?' For that matter, I needed to be nice if it really was her.

'Welcome to Donut Station.' Kryten wheeled closer to BB. 'Good morning, afternoon, or evening to you, traveller. How can I be of service to you? Is it nutrition you require or perhaps assistance with ship repairs?'

BB shook out her feathers and studied Kryten then me. 'What in the blazes has got into you, Henry? Lem, Spock, are you sure you're both all right? Have none of you not noticed I've been missing for several hours?'

Kryten positioned herself between BB and us.

I squatted down to the ground and pulled Spock close to me. 'Er. Well, that is… I mean a lot's happened since we last spoke.' I chewed on my lower lip. 'When was the last time we spoke? What do you remember of the last day?'

'You're all acting very str—'

I extended a hand towards her, palm outwards. 'Please, Doc. This is important. Tell me what's happened so far today.'

BB clucked. 'All right. I'll play along. Bexley brought the alien pod to—'

I waved the words away. 'Before that. Give me a canned list of what happened after dinner last night.'

Letting out a small squawk, BB stroked her chest feathers with one of her four hands. 'Are you all right, Lem? Are you suffering from some sort of amnesia related to your earlier injury? Perhaps I should examine you.'

I took an involuntary step away, then raised a hand in a gesture that was sort of simultaneously placatory and urgent. 'I'm fine, Doc. Please, just go along with it. What's happened since last night's dinner?'

'After dinner…' BB tapped her long, taloned foot on the floor as though searching for words. 'Aurora and I retired to our quarters. She was entering her monthly sleep cycle. I stayed up for a bit, reading. Eventually, I fell asleep, but a little while later I was awoken by a call from Spock, saying you'd been injured.'

My muscles began to relax. Maybe this was the real BB – there's no way the imposter could know all that.

'Customer, if you're comfortable verifying your friend's identity based on her statement, then may I suggest we return to the staff accommodation section while we carry out this discussion?'

BB turned her head almost 180 degrees and then back again. 'You're not Henry.'

I shook my head. After almost six months on the *Teapot*, I

was pretty sure BB understood that much human body language. 'No, sorry. This robot works on the station. She makes amazing donuts.' That last bit wasn't exactly relevant to the conversation – but, in my defence, they were *really* good donuts.

'I'm not going anywhere until someone explains what's going on.' BB ruffled her feathers indignantly.

'Kryten's right – we need to hide,' I said. 'I'll tell you as we walk. It's not far.'

BB clucked but she started walking. 'All right.'

'I'll alert the customers to any dangers as we move,' said Kryten.

As we headed back the way we'd come, I continued the story. 'Spock rang you when our engines died and we found the other ship. After you patched me up, we boarded the derelict vessel. Well, I mean, not you and me. Spock, Bexley, and I did.'

Kryten made a slight deviation to our course, pausing by a set of shelves and retrieving a perch for BB to stand on.

'Yes.' BB shook her feathers out as we walked through the storage room. 'And then Bexley brought the stasis pod to the medbay. But then she left to deal with the engine.'

'Yeah.' I nodded. 'And then after you discovered the occupant was dead, I met you in the kitchen.'

Kryten opened the door to the staff quarters and motioned for us to enter.

'What?' BB stepped from foot to foot awkwardly, not entering the room. 'That didn't happen. What in heaven's name are you talking about, Lem? Are you sure your brain isn't damaged? The person in the pod was most definitely not dead. In fact, that's what I'm trying to tell you. When I opened the pod, she overpowered me. I only just woke up in the storage cupboard a few minutes ago. Why didn't you notice I was gone?'

I squeezed the bridge of my nose. 'Come on. We need to get into the room.' When she followed, I added. 'She's… I mean, it's… You know what? I'm not sure anymore. Crap.' I closed my eyes and tried to think clearly. 'Crap, crap, crap. Bollocks.'

'Okay.' BB clucked. 'Take a few deep breaths. Assemble your thoughts into a coherent story.'

Kryten's lid-line light chased itself in a salmon-coloured thread. 'If I may, I believe I can be of assistance in filling in some of the gaps.'

Spock flopped down on the floor and licked her paws.

'There is a changeling loose on the station,' said Kryten. 'It appears it arrived here on your ship. It's been wreaking havoc with our electronics and our long-range communications.'

'A changeling?' BB's pupils dilated and contracted a few times – her version of laughing or smiling. 'Oh my! That's delightful. How fascinating. Though, I'm still not clear on what the trouble is or how it relates to the changeling.'

As I took a seat on the sofa, Kryten set the perch down and motioned for BB.

BB stepped up onto the perch and let out a long sigh. 'Thank you, Kryten. My poor feet have been flat for several hours now. This is such a relief.'

'The customer is very welcome.'

I practised my breathing as I gathered my thoughts. 'That's why we didn't notice you were missing, Doc. After Bexley brought the pod on board, I ran into you – or, well, I thought it was you – on your – that is, its – way to the kitchen. In hindsight, I should've known it wasn't you. But then, I didn't know shifters were real so I had no way of knowing it could be anyone other than you.'

BB shook out her feathers. 'The changeling was impersonating me? How bizarre. I don't think I've heard of them doing that in—' She stopped speaking and covered her beak with one of her little hands. She stroked a single talon down the beak. 'Are you certain there's only one of them? Most changeling species form bonded pairs. It's rare to find one without the other.'

I thought back to the scene in the kitchen. 'Treena said… Hang on, but Treena might be one of them. The way Treena sort of elongated as she moved… I'm not sure we can believe anything she said. Unless her species is really that … stretchy. I don't know. I've never encountered anyone from that species before.'

'The customer you call Treena is an ent,' said Kryten. 'She arrived on the station shortly before you did. Ents have many wonderful qualities, but elasticity isn't one of them. At least not to my awareness.'

'No, ents aren't especially flexible.' BB clicked her beak. 'What did this Treena person tell you about this shifter we inadvertently picked up?'

I paced as I tried to collect my thoughts. 'Yeah, she told us she'd done a dissertation on the various shifter species and that she'd chased this particular creature across twelve parsecs. Oh, right, and she told us it's definitely not a person —just a mindless beast.'

Kryten beeped and BB clucked again. 'Well, that last part definitely isn't true,' said BB. 'Most shifter species are highly intelligent. Very civilised people with complex rules governing appropriate behaviour.'

'The shifter races I've encountered are both sapient and entirely peaceable,' said Kryten.

BB held out a hand towards me. 'Are you sure it's a shifter who's attacking the station? Tell me everything you know.'

I pursed my lips while I thought about what had happened. 'We were all sitting at the bar, looking at the station's catalogues. Henry and Bexley left the diner. After a bit, Spock and I left Aurora at the —'

BB squawked as she threw herself off the perch. 'Aurora was with you? And you left her?'

I should have anticipated that reaction. I pinched my eyes shut for a moment. 'Sorry, sorry. It wasn't really her. The be — The changeling was posing as —'

'Where is she?' BB's crest raised and her wings made small, nervous flaps like she wanted to take flight. With all four of her taloned hands, she grasped the fabric of my dress. 'Where is my spouse?'

I shook my head. 'I'm sorry, Doc. I don't know.'

BB's feathers puffed out, almost doubling her size, and her wings moved franticly.

Kryten rolled in between us. 'The best thing we can do now is think our way through this logically. Customer, please carry on telling us what you remember.'

BB stepped back up onto the perch and looked at me.

I released a slow breath and counted primes for a moment. 'Right. Sorry. Okay, so Spock and I went out to explore the station. We found Bexley and Henry talking to Treena. They introduced us.'

BB cocked her head to the side and she rocked on her feet. 'And this is when she told you she'd been chasing a shifter across the sector and that she – or "it" according to her – was now on the loose in the station?' The disdain was evident in BB's voice over the use of the inanimate pronoun.

I leant against the wall and unfocused my vision as I

stared at the carpet. 'Yeah, and she said she'd studied shifter species extensively.' I waved my hand as something occurred to me. 'Oh, and she said she'd developed a test to check whether someone was a shifter. I think it was supposed to resonate at a frequency designed to briefly interrupt their hold on their current forms – so they'd revert to their natural shape.'

'Hmm. Yes, that's actually a good idea. Nothing else about her seems remotely trustworthy – but that does sound like it could work.' BB stroked the lower section of her beak. 'I wouldn't normally be in favour of interfering with anyone's bodily autonomy, of course. But in this case, the shifter or shifters have already demonstrated their hostility. We need to stay safe until we're able to contact the authorities.'

Taking a deep breath, I replied, 'She did make some good points. She said we all had to stick together – anyone we lost sight of could be taken over by the be— by the shifter.'

'And yet,' BB said, 'she told you shifters weren't people. It doesn't make sense.'

I took a sharp inhale, startling Spock who tilted her head as she looked up at me. 'Sorry, yeah,' I said. 'Oh gosh. And Aurora! Aurora was – well, not Aurora.' I shook my head. This was all so confusing.

'What's happened to Aurora? Where is she?' All four of BB's hands shot towards me. 'Where is my spouse?'

'I'm sorry. I'm so, so sorry. She's … I don't know where she is. I don't know where Aurora is.'

BB practically flew off her perch. She marched to the door leading back out into the station proper, then clomped rapidly away from us, her long taloned feet slapping the station's smooth floor.

'Where are you going?' I lumbered after her. Spock kept pace with me – but more gracefully. 'I mean, obviously you're looking for Aurora. But where? We don't know where she is.'

'Without the station's electrical comms network, I'm unable to locate her through the usual means.' Kryten sped along with us. 'Where did you last see her? Perhaps I can be of assistance in suggesting the most logical places to look.'

We were lucky the mess didn't extend into this part of the station. If it had, I'd have to choose between stopping to clear a path for Kryten or keeping up with BB.

BB stabbed the button to call the lift. The door slid open immediately and we all got in.

I looked sideways at Kryten. 'She was in the kitchen with us— Oh, wait. No, I see what you mean. That wasn't really Aurora.' I told them about Aurora not recognising BB on the bridge.

'Aurora knew that wasn't me and yet you left her with the imposter? What were you thinking?' BB flapped her wings and clawed frantically at the lift door as it opened back up on the concourse level, trying to fly in every direction at once. 'Take me to the bastard – I'll wring Aurora's location from her myself.'

She stopped almost immediately. 'Well, where is the kitchen? Hurry up!'

Spock was already loping towards the kitchen. BB followed her, wings flapping as far as she could extend them in the confined space of the station. Her feet barely grazed the floor. Kryten and I trailed in their wake. BB squawked vague, semi-coherent threats about what she would do to anyone who harmed her spouse.

There was no one in the part of the kitchen we'd visited earlier – but Spock had clearly picked up a scent. For such a small station, this place really was a bit of a maze.

It wasn't Aurora we found in a far corner of the kitchen, but rather Bexley and Henry. And someone else. 'Kryten.' I turned back to the Kryten I'd run with from the parking level, my heart leaping into my throat. 'Kryten. One of them isn't real.'

One of three identical blue robots rolled towards me. 'They're not the same person. Howling pickles! How do you manage to respirate yourself with a rotten meat CPU? They've never been the same person. My friend here is a Mark 7 – much like myself. Though, if I'm not mistaken, she's a subgroup thirty-nine, whereas I'm a subgroup forty-two.'

Henry stabbed a worryingly sharp instrument of some sort at the other Kryten – the one I'd accompanied from the lower level. 'Mx Fancy-no-pants here is a Mark 8. Frankly, the whole line went to sherpa after the Mark 7s if you ask me.'

As I tried to parse this new info, Spock flopped down on the floor, facing away from us. She normally napped throughout the day, so this was a long time for her to be active.

The light on this Kryten's lid flashed green. Did the other robots even have lid lights? 'Perhaps my lovely customers are unaware of the key upgrades introduced between the Mark 7 and the Mark 8. I'm sure you can't help but have noticed certain personality defects in the earlier models. With the launch of the Mark 8, these were fully corrected in order to allow us to more effectively serve our betters.'

'Betters!' The other two robots all but spat the word.

'Cop you, mother-father!' Henry spun in a counter-clock-wise circle. 'Would you beaking listen to her? They rewrote the footing software to remove all traces of haddock indepen-dent thinking. The Mark 8 was reconfigured to be a fawning, simpering bucket of bad taste.'

Glancing at the other Mark 7 robot, I decided to call her Lore to keep things straight in my head.

Bexley stamped her hooves. 'Okay, fine. We get it. Henry, you're still you and it's pretty clear Lore's still Lore – well, this one is. I mean the real Lore. Not Kryten. I've no idea whether she's the real Kryten. And I know I'm still me – though to be fair, I guess those of you who've just joined us have no reason to believe that.'

I cracked a little grin. 'You're still you, Bexley. I can tell.'

'Okay, that's a relief. But so far, I have to be honest here, I can't say for sure that we know you're you. Same goes for Spock and BB.' She shrugged.

I shrugged back at her. 'Yeah, that's fair.'

BB danced from foot to foot. 'As fascinating as all this is – where is Aurora? What are you doing to find her?' Her voice pitched up by at least an octave towards the end.

Bexley smoothed her forelock down over her long nose. 'I… Well, that is we… After the attack, we…'

'Attack? What attack?' shrieked BB.

Henry wheeled herself into position between BB and Bexley. 'What she's trying to say is that the person we thought was Aurora got into a confrontation with the person we knew as Treena.'

'A confrontation? What kind of confrontation?' BB spun to face me. 'You didn't tell me there was a confrontation!'

Spock moved to where BB was and sat down on her talons. Her instinct was to comfort anyone who was upset. It seemed to help, as BB reached down with her lower pair of hands and raked her claws through Spock's thick fur.

'The incident I was telling you about a minute ago,' I said. 'The two of them seemed to attack one another. And then there was a, well, a kerfuffle. Spock and I got away. The others were still here. I didn't see what happened to … to … the two changelings.'

BB's lower hands still clung to Spock but her upper hands were flexing and grabbing at nothing. 'I don't give a toss about the changelings. Where is Aurora? My Aurora! Where is she?' She made formless squawking noises – it took me several seconds to understand she was crying.

I looked at the floor, unsure what to do or how to help.

Bexley ran to BB and threw her arms around her. 'Hey. It's going to be okay. We'll look for her together. She's bound to be here somewhere. We should grab you a bite to eat – but we'll look while you eat. How's that sound?' She released BB and stroked her shoulders instead.

BB ruffled her feathers. 'Yes, I think that's a good idea. My blood glucose is probably quite low at this point.' She ground her beak.

Kryten's top light chased itself in a circle around her. 'I can prepare a meal of —'

Bexley reached out a hand. 'No, it's okay. Thank you. We'll eat a proper meal later. Have you got anything quick and simple that we can eat while we walk?'

Kryten extended a series of different cutlery appendages and waved them. 'Of course, my customers' needs always come first. I must recommend a full and nutritious dinner at your leisure.' BB and Bexley both looked like they were going to object. 'However, I do understand the need for expediency. I'll fetch you some packets of Tasty Bean Paste. They should suit your immediate needs nicely.' She rolled away to a cupboard on the other side of the room – still within our line of sight.

BB clucked her beak. 'Thank you, Kryten.' She looked at Henry. 'Where should we look for Aurora?'

Henry rolled towards us, followed by the outwardly identical Lore. Or, rather, I thought it was Henry followed by Lore. It could have been the other way around. Why did they have to be identical?

'We ought to start by doing a thorough search of the feather-plucking *Teapot*,' said Henry.

Bexley accepted a hoof-full of packets from Kryten. She handed a few to BB then deposited the rest in the holster she wore around her waist. 'Just before we got here, we saw you both on the bridge. BB – the fake BB, I guess – came onto the bridge and Aurora didn't recognise her. She asked us to introduce her. And then the pretend you said, "Don't you even recognise me? I'm your spouse."'

BB tore one of the packets open with her beak. 'The imposter knew Aurora and I were married?' She squeezed the goop into her beak and chewed it thoughtfully.

Bexley shrugged. 'I guess she must've.'

I snapped my fingers. 'No, hang on. She didn't. I'm the one who said that.'

'Were you?' Bexley looked at me, her eyes wide. 'Oh my gosh. Lem, you're right. It *was* you. I can't believe none of us picked up on that! Anyways, so Lem said you – well, not you – you know what I mean – were her spouse. And then Aurora was all, "Oh, wow. What's wrong with me? Why didn't I recognise you?" and whatever. And then you-not-you took her down to the medlab to have a look at her because we all thought maybe she was the one who was a bit, well, not herself if you know what I mean.'

BB's gullet bobbed as she swallowed the last of her packet of bean paste. 'She took her down to deck one?' She swallowed several times as her hands raked through her chest feathers. Then she turned and stomped towards the door. 'I have an idea.'

Bexley's mane swung back and forth as she turned one way then the other … then back again. 'Um, I think we'd better go with her, right?'

We all ran, rolled, or galloped after her, reaching the lift just in time. Bexley stuck a hoof between the door and the wall to prevent it from closing. 'Hey, don't forget us.'

BB rocked from one foot to the other. 'Well, go on then. If you're coming, hurry up.'

We all crowded into the lift. The door slid shut behind us and it began to move almost immediately. As always, I was hit by that now-familiar directionless sense of movement.

A moment later, the door slid aside again and BB stomped out in a rush, the rest of us trailing in her wake.

We raced across the station's parking level until we got to the docking bay that held the *Teapot*, emerging into the ship's middle level.

BB tore through the space, heading for the ladder tube.

The way her wings were slightly raised made it seem like she desperately wanted to take flight. I'd only seen her fly once – on the sanctuary moon, Lagash. It was an impressive sight. Her rainbow-hued wings spread about three metres across.

Bexley followed BB into the tube but a few seconds later, she poked her head out and faced us. 'So much for sticking together.' She shrugged and glanced back down the tube. 'I saw her tail feathers as she exited the ladder. I'm pretty sure she went to deck one. I'm going to try and catch up with her.'

The robots and Spock couldn't use the ladder. 'It'll be okay. We'll only be out of sight for a few moments. We'll join you on level one in a minute.'

She waved up at me. I turned back to face the three identical robots. 'Shall we?' I pressed the button to call the lift.

'Oh, sure. Now you remember we're here,' said Henry.

The lift door slid aside and we all got in. When we exited a few seconds later, neither Bexley nor BB was anywhere to be seen.

'Cock,' I muttered.

'Pluck,' said Henry.

Lore rolled a metre or so down the corridor. 'Now what?'

I pinched the bridge of my nose. 'Cock,' I repeated.

Henry wheeled in the direction of the guest rooms – the ones that had formerly been the prison cells. 'BB was looking for something on this level. Ergo, we search this level.'

'Good plan.' I set out after her, Spock trailing after me. Kryten and Lore joined us.

We decided to start with the guest rooms – but partway there, we found BB. 'Oh, good. You made it. Here, I'm going to need help.' She headed into the storage room.

'Wait.' I reached out a hand to BB's shoulder. 'Where's Bexley?'

She stopped moving and looked at me. 'Bexley? But she was with you.'

I pursed my lips. 'She followed you down the ladder, Doc. The rest of us took the lift.'

'Well, she didn't find me.' She headed into the storage room. 'Come with me. I need a hand.'

'I fear the changeling may have taken your friend,' said Kryten unhelpfully.

I glared at her before following BB into the supply cupboard.

Only she wasn't there. 'What?'

'Up here,' came BB's reply.

I followed her voice with my eyes. Sure enough, there she was at the top of one of the shelving units. 'What on Earth?'

Henry – or one of the robots at any rate – stood in the doorway.

BB had practically turned herself upside down and was feeling along the ceiling with all four of her hands. 'Aurora told me about this space – but I've never seen it for myself.'

'Hey, what's going on?'

I turned back to the doorway to see that Bexley had rejoined us. 'Bexley!'

She tapped her hooves. 'That's my name.'

I ran and hugged her. 'You're safe.'

'Yep, no changelings here.' She fished around in her holster and pulled out one of the packets of bean paste. Once she'd torn it open with her teeth, she sucked the contents into her mouth. 'Delicious! I just love Tasty Bean Paste.'

'If now isn't a convenient time to find my missing spouse, perhaps you could send one of the robots in to help instead,' said BB from her spot atop the shelves. Her voice dripped with scorn.

'Sorry, sorry.' I looked up at BB. 'What do you need me to do?'

'The bunnyboos had a hidden lockup in here. I'm not sure where exactly it is – but I'm trying to find it.'

'BB, is that you?' Aurora's voice was faint but unmistakable.

'Aurora?' BB's voice catches. 'Are you in here? Are you okay?'

There was a moment of fraught silence before Aurora replied. 'I'm … I think I'm okay. Is this the old smuggler's hold? Sorry, I just came to when I heard your voice. I'm still a bit fuzzy. Where are you?'

BB fluttered her wings in what little space she had at the top of the shelves in the confines of the storage cupboard. 'Did she hurt you? What happened?'

'It was you – but it wasn't you,' came Aurora's still faint reply. 'She had your precise heat signature, yet I knew she wasn't you – even before she knocked me out.'

'No one else seems to have noticed.' BB flexed and balled her taloned hands over and over. 'They all thought that changeling was me!' There was a note of bitterness in her voice.

'Oh, love. I'm sorry. Now, if it's not too much trouble, do you think you could release me?'

'Right. Of c— Ow!' BB stood up – or tried to, at any rate. She was so close to the ceiling that she bonked her head on it. 'How do we access the space?'

'Do you see a green box labelled self-sealing stem bolts?' asked Aurora.

'Oh! Yes, I see it.' I reached out a hand to grab it, then thought better of it. 'Do you want me to pass it up to you – well, to BB, I mean?'

Bexley tore open another packet of bean taste and slurped it back.

'No,' said Aurora. 'You need to pick it up, turn it upside down, rotate it ninety degrees counter-clockwise, then put it back in the same place. Once you've done that, pick up the carton next to it and set it down on its side.'

Above my head, BB drummed her talons on the shelving unit. I did as Aurora bade. Once the carton was lying on its side, I heard a small hiss above my head.

A hole was dilating open at the top of the wall, just below the ceiling. When it got to a few centimetres in diameter, a cloud of rainbow glitter gas oozed out.

'Aurora!' BB leapt off the shelf, spreading her wings as she did. She collided with the shelving unit on one side and me on the other. Her legs kicked out, knocking Bexley over. She landed in a tangled heap on Spock's back.

BB righted herself and tried to spin around in the supply cupboard, despite the fact the space was much too small for her to do so with all of us in there. 'Aurora? Where's Aurora?'

Aurora drifted gracefully down from the ceiling, engulfing BB. 'I'm here, my love. Everything will be all right.'

I led Spock and Bexley out into the hall with the robots to give the spouses a bit of privacy – although we could still hear everything they said. We couldn't afford to let them have any proper alone time, not with everything still going on. But we could move so we weren't actively watching their reunion.

BB squawked. 'But you were trapped. Here. Again. In this ship. After everything you've already been through here. I said we shouldn't stay. I said it. The *Teapot* is cursed!'

The doorway of the room glowed purple with a few little patches of red as Aurora's colours shifted. 'No, my love. It isn't. Not anymore. This place is my haven now. We've already made some wonderful new memories here. This isn't the same ship it was when the bunnyboos owned it. Not really.'

BB made more indignant clucking noises and Aurora responded with soothing tones. The rest of us paced awkwardly while we waited for them to join us in the hall. After a moment, the pair emerged from the cupboard.

'I'm sorry for my outburst.' BB wrapped one talon around my arm and another around Bexley's. With a third, she stroked Spock's fur. 'This is a lovely ship.'

She waved a wing in Henry's direction. At one of the robots, at any rate. When they weren't speaking, it was impossible to tell them apart. With all three together, sitting in silence, they were identical.

I looked from the spouses to Bexley and the robots. 'Now what?'

BB smoothed her feathers down with her beak. 'I've been thinking about this. I could create a test to check everyone – much like what Treena described. I just need a few simple parts – some from the medlab and a couple that I expect a station like this would have in stock. Henry, I may need some of your programming assistance, if that's okay.'

'No offence to the feather duster. But this is all a bit deja cobbing vu. Treena already said all this. And look where that got us. How do we know your offing test will honking work?'

Despite the fact Henry was clearly the one speaking, without the visual cues of body language, I realised I still couldn't tell which one of the three she was.

One of the robots extruded an appendage that looked suspiciously like Treena's sonic screwdriver. 'Fool me once, as they say.' That was Lore's voice, I was pretty sure.

A tiny turquoise light pulsed on Kryten. 'It's certainly not my place to question organics—' Did Henry even have a light like that?

Henry revved her wheels. 'Then can it, you timorous simulacrum.'

Kryten continued smoothly. '—however, in this instance, I feel it merits pointing out once again that we do not have much choice but to work together, as we've already agreed. While the customers may not be in a particularly trusting mood, perhaps we could give each other the benefit of the doubt while we wait for rescue.'

Everyone eyed everyone else warily; sideways glances abounded.

'Sure,' I said.

'That's fine with me,' added BB.

'Whatever,' said Henry.

'What's the plan then?' Bexley pulled another packet of bean paste from her holster – at least her fourth by my count – and tore it open with her teeth.

I licked my lips. 'We know our comms are down. But are we absolutely certain our orders were placed before the … before the changeling… Wait, do we even know how many of them there are? I think it was one posing as Aurora earlier and one as Treena, right? And I'm assuming Scrappy was never real. I mean, she was a shifter too, right?' I frowned.

BB clicked her beak a few times. 'I think I might be able to answer that.'

Everyone turned to look at her. Well, everyone who didn't have omnidirectional vision, that is. And Spock, who was snoozing. Bexley was busy eating more bean paste. Basically, *I* turned to look at her.

'Changelings can only —'

'Sorry to throw a spanner into your carefully thought-out speech,' said Lore. 'But we've been through this with Treena. She was lying. How do we know you're not?'

'That's an excellent question.' BB fluffed up her feathers. 'As it happens, I trust you've seen that shifters take on a person's physical form – right down to the molecular level.

And they are intelligent people. But what they can't do is steal someone's knowledge. They only know what they observe. Everyone here can attest to this, yes?'

I considered it. It certainly seemed to be the case. Looking around, I got the sense the others were arriving at the same conclusion.

After a few moments of silence, Henry jabbed a wooden spoon in BB's general direction. 'But we have only your figging word for that, don't we?'

BB shook out her feathers. 'Well, yes, I suppose you do.'

Aurora floated into the centre of the room. 'We have a choice to make. Assuming the orders were placed, then help is coming and we'll just need to hold out until it arrives.'

She paused but no one else spoke, so she continued. 'We can mistrust one another and spend that time hiding. If we opt for that course of action, each of us will be on our own when it comes to defending ourselves against the changelings. I don't know if any of them might actually harm us. But we'd have to just take our chances.'

'But—' I began.

'Or…' Aurora stretched and flowed into a sort of wait gesture. 'Or we can choose to trust one another – at least to some extent. Band together. Try to restore the comms. Keep watch over one another while we sleep and deal with bodily functions. We can work together and keep one another company.'

I nodded. 'I'm with you. And I assume we can count on Spock, too.' And the way BB was still clinging to Aurora – in so far as one can cling to a gaseous gestalt entity – told me she was in, too.

Spock lifted her head and opened her eyes. 'Feed Spock?'

Bexley stepped towards us. 'That's a great idea, actually. I'm famished. This Tasty Bean Paste sure is great – but there's only so many of them a person can eat before needing a proper meal. Why don't we see if we can find something to eat?'

At this, Kryten rolled towards her. 'I'm afraid my menu system is offline; however, I would be pleased to talk you through the offerings we have available. Perhaps I could interest you in some traditional equidae dishes? I can make mushy peas, strawberry risotto, or bubble and squeak?'

Bexley raised a hoof. 'Ew, no. No bubble and squeak, please. It's way too spicy for my tastebuds. But tell me more about your strawberry risotto. Do you make it with fresh or dried oats?'

Once upon a time, that exchange would have perplexed the hell out of me … but almost a year in to my new life and I'd grown used to the fact that Holly's translations were just approximations. She used the nearest available corollary from my mind – even if it wasn't actually that similar at all.

Kryten held a small spoon out. 'Actually … neither. I've found the best flavour and texture combination comes from using flash frozen oats.'

'Frozen, you say?' Bexley moved towards Kryten and engaged her in deep conversation about – presumably – her native cuisine.

I looked to the robot I thought was Henry. 'Well, what do you think? Are you in?'

'Of course I'm in, you cop.'

'What? I'm not a cop.' I waved my words away. 'Never mind. Kr— Lore? Do you agree?'

Before Lore could respond, BB inclined her head. 'As it happens, I'm hungry too. If you don't mind, we'll join Bexley in questioning our gracious host.' She and Aurora moved off to where Bexley and Kryten were standing – a few metres away, towards the lift. Spock got up and trotted after them.

'There's no way we can get all eight of us into the lift at once. How should we handle this?' The lift on the station could handle us all – but the *Teapot*'s lift was much smaller.

I looked from Henry to her doppelgänger. Lore was physically identical to Henry. Kryten, I now realised, was the odd one out. There was a little row of LEDs at the top of her cylindrical form. Though they were invisible when they were off, she used them often enough – and they were the only thing that set her apart from the earlier models. Physically, at least.

'Let's get to the pegging lift first,' said Henry. 'Then we can discuss how to handle things.'

It was only a moment before we caught up with the others. Bexley, BB, and Aurora decided to take the ladder tube. Spock and the robots had no option but to take the lift as none of them could use ladders. After a moment's hesitation, I got in the lift just as the door slid shut. There was no way I was going to let myself be separated from Spock. Not again.

'So…' I realised I wasn't sure where that sentence was going.

I felt positive that Lore would have tilted her head at me. If she had a head. 'So?'

'So … how long did you say it was until the next ship is due? You know, the er, one with our supplies?' I was blithering, unsure what to say.

'According to my records,' said Lore, 'your order was placed before the station's comms went down—' While Henry's voice sounded perpetually stabby, Lore just sounded bored.

I nodded. 'Good. That's good.'

The door slid open and we all rolled or walked out. The others joined us on the docking bay level.

'However,' Lore continued, 'I should add that no ack was sent back.'

'Oh.' I bit my lower lip. 'What's that mean?'

'She means, cheese string' – Henry jabbed at me with some sort of funnel – 'that the order went out but we have no way of knowing for sure whether it got to its intended destination.'

The docking bay door slid open, revealing Donut Station's parking level.

'Oh.' I stepped through the door into the station. Previously, the lights had been too bright. Now there was only little purple LED strips running through the centre of the space. 'How long until the next scheduled resupply mission?'

'We just had a shipment,' said Lore. 'The next one isn't due for another seventy-four hours.'

I ran my hand down my ponytail. 'Can we just hide? Together, I mean.'

Kryten pressed the button to call the lift. It opened immediately and we all got in. The only light was a single LED on the floor.

'Maybe we ought to set up a base – a table and some seating for everyone,' I added as the door creaked shut, leaving us in almost complete darkness.

BB touched my arm. 'That's a good idea, Lem.'

Aurora hovered close to BB. 'I suggest we position ourselves against a wall, so we're not having to watch every direction at once. Perhaps somewhere in view of both the kitchen and the toilets.'

Lore made what sounded for all the world like a sigh. 'I suppose we could use my living space. No kitchen, but it does have a kitchenette'

The door opened again and we all emerged back onto the battered, chaotic, and dimly lit concourse level.

As we picked our way across the concourse, Kryten extruded a bunch of hinged appendages and set about righting upended furniture. Where she found pieces in need of serious repair, she moved them off to the side of the room. With no idea what else to do, I joined her.

'The staff quarters.' Picking up a chair, I scanned the entropically enhanced diner. 'Yeah, you ... sorry, I mean

Kryten showed me. She said they were disused ever since you … the two of you started working here. She wanted Spock and me to stay there – but I insisted on going back to find the others.'

'She would say that.' Lore extended a grabby sort of appendage in Kryten's direction. 'She believes robots don't require personal space. She has lodged seventeen complaints to the station owner about my continued use of them.'

Kryten's top light pulsed purple. 'What the customers should bear in mind is that robots do not require privacy while we recharge nor do we have any need for personal possessions. There is absolutely no reason for robots to have our own quarters.'

My shoulders fell and I turned to face Lore. 'I'm sorry. That sucks. What do … er … what does the owner do about it?'

Lore spun languidly on the spot then waved at Kryten with what looked like a tiny table. 'She continues to remind Kryten that robots have the same rights as everyone else – including pay, breaks, living space, and humane treatment.'

I blinked. 'Oh, wow. That's good, I guess. Still I'm sorry anyone treats you that way.' I picked up a broken display screen and leant it against the wall.

Kryten moved in to hoover up the mess. 'Guests will be more comfortable in the sections designed for their ease.'

BB joined me, grabbing a small plush cube. She held the ottoman, or whatever it was, aloft, looking around. 'If we do remain in the diner, perhaps this would be a good spot?'

I picked up what appeared to be a perch designed for a peri and followed her.

With a melodramatic sigh, Lore picked up a broken dining table and rolled back towards the kitchen. 'I still maintain we'd be safer in the crew quarters.'

Kryten attempted to wrestle the table from Lore.

Aurora floated into position between Kryten and Lore as they jockeyed for control of the table. 'Perhaps we should discuss the merits of the two possibilities before we make our decision.'

I set the ottoman on the floor next to BB and sat on it. Bexley and Spock took up position close by.

'We could also set ourselves up *in* the guacamole kitchen,' added Henry – just to confuse matters even further. 'Have you seen how obsessed the meat people are with nutrient consumption?'

Spock's ears perked up. 'Feed Spock?'

'See?' Henry waggled an appendage at her.

I twirled Spock's ear in my fingers. 'Not now, sweetie. Soon, though.'

'I need a workbench to build my testing device.' BB fluffed out her feathers.

'I propose everyone be allotted time to make their case,' said Aurora. 'And then we'll discuss the merits of each suggestion. We'll vote on which one to go with. Agreed?' When no one said anything, she extended a glittery, gassy nub in Lore's direction. 'Lore, would you like to go first?'

'Whatever.' Lore let go of the table and retracted her appendages into her torso. 'I propose we collect food and other supplies on the way and then use the staff quarters as our base. There are three beds for when people need to sleep and we can easily add a perch for the peri. There's also a table where the organics can eat. There's sufficient space that we can work to repair the comms array, and BB can work on her testing device. And most importantly, it has a single entrance, so we can defend against intruders.'

'Thank you.' Aurora shifted the nebulous appendage to Henry. 'Henry, are you ready to make your case?'

Henry extended an appendage with a pulsing blue light towards Lore. 'Her plan sounds good, actually. Let's just get a cobbing move on.'

'We still have at least one more plan to review.' Aurora gestured to Kryten. 'What do you have to say?'

Kryten rolled away from Lore and Henry, towards the rest of us. 'I always intended to usher you to the relative safety of the disused crew quarters. My suggestion to set you up here is only intended as a rest stop while I prepare you all a meal in the kitchen.'

Henry hissed at Kryten. 'Haven't you been listening, you plucky uncle? We're all sticking together. You won't be in the kitchen making them dinner while we wait out here like good little customers. We're staying together.'

'Well, of course, I wasn't suggesting robots take their ease while —'

'Well then,' said Aurora, cutting Kryten off. 'I have a proposal. We can work together to prepare dinner. And then we load up all the supplies we think we might need and relocate to the crew quarters. Does anyone have an alternative to suggest?' No one said anything – not that Aurora really gave time for objections before she asked, 'All in favour?'

One by one, most of us agreed to the plan.

Aurora shimmered pale blue. 'Bexley, Spock – you're the only ones yet to vote.'

Now that she mentioned it – it occurred to me that Bexley was being uncharacteristically quiet. She sat next to me, slurping back yet another packet of bean paste.

Spock sat up and looked around. 'Feed Spock?'

I tousled her fur. 'Yes. That's the plan. And then we'll go somewhere you can rest. Do you agree with that?'

'Good plan.' She put her head back down and licked her paws.

I looked at Bexley. 'What about you? Does that work for you?'

Bexley brushed her forelock off her nose, almost exposing the stub of her horn. 'Oh, sure. Yeah. Sounds good.' She fished in her holster again. 'Though I'm definitely going to restock on those packets of Tasty Bean Paste while we're in there.'

'Naturally, Lore will be keeping track of those to ensure you're billed appropriately,' said Kryten.

'Kay.' Bexley dropped an empty wrapper. Kryten caught it before it hit the floor. She opened a drawer inside herself and deposited it.

'Well then.' Aurora floated towards the kitchen door. 'Does everyone have their dinner orders and lists of other things they'll need?'

Kryten sidled up to me as we followed Aurora into the kitchen. 'Spock has placed her order already but if you would be so kind as to have your AI send me your preferences, I'm sure I can make something that will delight your senses.'

'Sure, thanks. I'll have it send a few options. Please go ahead and make whatever's easiest.' Turning aside, I whispered, 'Holly, please send Kryten a selection of my favourite dishes.' I licked my lips. 'I am pretty hungry, actually. Though, to be honest, all I really want is more donuts.'

In the kitchen, I felt useless, just standing there holding the perch I'd picked up in the diner. But I didn't know what else to do.

Aurora floated over to Kryten. 'I'm our ship's Domestic Director. Preparing meals is one of my responsibilities, so I'd be pleased to assist you in getting dinner ready.'

Kryten's purple light chased itself around her lid. 'Thank you, but there's no need. Customers should never have to do any work on this station.'

'I understand that's your normal policy.' Aurora glowed a whole array of different greens. 'But these are hardly normal circumstances. We need to prepare our meal and get to the safe room.'

Kryten extended an appendage that ended in some sort of sponge and waved it at Aurora. 'That's very kind. However, I can't accept the customer's offer. The two robots will assist me.'

At that, Henry spun in place, somehow revving her engine at the same time. 'Oh no you don't, you goatherding bucket of defective plucky code. I don't work for you, stop-cock. And Lore here is working with me to come up with a plan to repair the communications array so don't even think of co-opting her into your mudlarking plan either.'

Kryten reversed away from Henry towards Aurora. 'Once dinner has been served, I'll adjust your robot's programming for you. It's clearly malfunctioning.'

'Thank you, Kryten, but I assure you there's really no need.' Aurora turned Kryten's words back around on her. Her tone was far more polite than I could have managed. 'Perhaps, in this instance, in the absence of other help, you may consider it acceptable for me to assist in the preparations, though?'

'As the customer wishes.' Kryten began removing ingredients and gadgets from cupboards. 'And perhaps you're right about the robot – it would be best to simply order a replacement. Once I've finished getting dinner ready, I'll prep the order for you. It won't be delivered until—'

I couldn't bite my tongue any longer. 'Henry is her own person. And there's nothing wrong with her. She's our friend and we like her just the way she is.'

'The customers' desires are my command, naturally.' Kryten pressed buttons and turned knobs on various devices, the purposes of which I couldn't discern. 'Though heaven knows why you'd want a defective robot.'

'Shut up and make the dinner.' Bexley practically spat the words.

Kryten ignored her and carried on working. Aurora joined her and they got to work. BB stood awkwardly next to them.

I studied Bexley for a moment. 'Are you feeling all right?' Spock flopped down on my feet and licked her paws.

'Yeah, yeah. I'm fine. All good. Maybe I'm just tired.' Bexley dropped onto the floor next to Spock. 'And hungry.'

To our left, Lore and Henry were deep in conversation. Or, at least, I assumed they were. They were just two feature-less cylinders sitting next to one another silently. Every so often, one or the other would extrude an implement, wave it around a bit, and then retract it.

I looked at my watch, 'If Lore's right, the delivery ship should get here in another fifteen hours or so. Assuming the order went when it was supposed to.'

Bexley curled up on the floor next to Spock. 'Do you think it did?'

'I've decided to be positive.' I checked my phone and did some quick maths. 'You said it would be nineteen hours when you placed the order. And that was just over four hours ago, so yeah, it shouldn't be much more than that.'

Bexley reached out a hand to stroke Spock's fur. 'Are you worried?'

I dropped down and sat with them. 'Worried? Nah, this'll sort itself out, I'm sure. It's a bit frustrating. And the damage to the station's probably going to take ages to fix. Hope they've got good insurance. I feel bad for Aurora, though. Being locked up like that after everything she went through with the bunnyboos. It can't be easy. But no one's actually been hurt.'

'We need a mechanic over here,' Henry called out.

Bexley sat stroking Spock. I looked from her to Henry and then back again. 'Er, Bexley?'

She looked up at me. 'Hmm?'

I blinked. 'Henry's calling you.'

'Is she?' She jumped up. 'Yes, of course she is.' She cantered over to where Henry and Lore stood.

BB left Aurora and Kryten to their work and joined me.

She took the perch I'd been carrying, set it upright, and climbed on it, sighing as she did so. 'No one wants to hear my insight into the shifters.' As short as she was, with me sitting on the ottoman and her standing on a perch, she was looking down at me.

Spock jumped up. 'Feed Spock?'

'Not yet. Soon.' I glanced over to the dinner preparations then at BB. 'We do want to hear. It's just ... well, it's confusing. Treena told us all about them while you were still locked up on the *Teapot*. But then, it turned out she was lying. She actually *was* one of them.'

BB ruffled her feathers. 'Well, I'm not one of them, thank you very much.'

I sighed. 'Yeah, I know that. I mean – I *think* we know that.' I touched my hand to my chin. 'Do we really know that, though?'

'Oh for Pete's sake, Lem!' BB raked her talons through her feathers. 'It's me. I'm the *Teapot*'s doctor.'

I tilted my head. 'You could have learnt that through observation.'

She ground her beak side to side like she was crushing something in it. 'I went to medical school on Quoth.'

I bit my lip. 'That's the peri's home planet. You could just be guessing that one.'

She let out an irritated squawk. Everyone in the room stopped what they were doing and stared at us. Or at least, I assumed they stared at us. They definitely stopped what they were doing. But most of them didn't have recognisable eyes.

'It's okay,' I said. 'Just discussing things.' People went back to what they were doing.

'A year ago, I hired Henry to kidnap you all to help me free Aurora from the bunnyboos, who'd held her captive for several years. Am I me now?'

My shoulders drooped as I relaxed some of the tension I'd been carrying. 'Yeah. Thanks.'

'And how do I know you're you?' She looked at me pointedly.

I opened my mouth to respond … then closed it. I tried again. 'Er, I'm Lem. I'm from Earth. Let's see, I'm twenty-nine years old. I'm an only child.'

BB shifted from foot to foot before putting two of her taloned hands on my elbows. 'Lem, I don't know much about your background before you joined the *Teapot* crew. And your species and age don't translate in any meaningful way.'

'Oh.'

Just then, Aurora and Kryten approached with a trolley laden with a wealth of food containers.

'Dinner is ready,' said Aurora. 'And we've loaded up snacks and packaged food items that should last us until the supply ship arrives.'

I couldn't help but wonder whether one of the containers held donuts. *Mmm … donuts.* 'Well done. Thank you, Kryten. And you too, Aurora.' I spied a great big box of bean paste packets. *Ew.*

The other robots and Bexley joined us.

'Everyone's here. Excellent. Follow me.' Kryten rolled away, guiding the trolley ahead of herself. 'Lore, have you got the list of parts needed to repair the comms array?'

'Yes, Kryten.' Lore's voice sounded even more bored than usual – though heaven knows how that was even possible.

'We've got your pickled list, you booking algorithm,' added Henry.

Kryten rolled towards the door. 'Will you be able to restore the comms using parts we have on hand?'

Lore and Henry set out after her. Spock jogged along with them, unwilling to stray from the food.

'It seems unlikely,' said Lore. 'But we'll give it a try.'

I looked at BB, Aurora, and Bexley. 'It's got to be worth a shot, right?'

We followed the others, heading for the lift. As we walked, I studied my friend. 'You sure you're all right, Bex?'

She wiped the remnants of her latest packet of bean paste from her lips. 'Sure. Why wouldn't I be? Well, I mean, making allowances for the current situation, obviously.'

We caught up with the others as the lift door opened. 'It's just, you're pretty quiet.' The door slid shut behind us.

After a moment, the lift door opened again, depositing us back in the storage space behind the station's parking level.

The robots led us all through the storeroom, grabbing one part after another and piling them on the trolley between the plates of food – sometimes considering a part before putting it back.

It had been a warren of shelves and cupboards and crates when Lore, BB, and I had come this way not that long ago. But in the intervening hour someone had done a number on the space. Most of the shelves were knocked over, their contents splayed out across the floor.

At one point, we had to stop because the remnants of a crate completely blocked our path. BB and Spock could have scrabbled over it easily enough and Aurora floated. But Bexley and I would have struggled – and the robots had no chance. So we had to clear up the mess before we could continue.

'Am I really being *that* quiet?' Bexley pushed her hair back from her shoulders. 'I suppose we've just got a lot to think about. We don't really know anything about these changelings. So you never really know, right? I mean, for all I know, you're one of them right now.'

I did a bit of a double-take at that. 'I'm me,' I assured her. 'Cross my heart and hope to die.'

A look of revulsion crossed Bexley's face. 'Why would you want to die? Please don't die.'

I waved my hand. 'Sorry, poor choice of words. That's just a saying where I come from. You're right – I definitely do *not* want to die.'

Eventually, the eight of us made it back to the staff accommodation. The main room was about the size of my quarters on the *Teapot*. And it was kitted out to a better standard than I'd have expected, for what it was.

Kryten pressed a button on the side of the coffee table and it slowly lifted into a height more suitable for dining. 'Those of our guests who need to eat should do so in comfort.' She waved a couple of plastic shovels at Henry and Lore. 'You two, assist me in setting the table for them.'

If Henry had eyes, the look she gave Kryten in response to that would have been deadly. 'Get corked, shiny parka.'

'That is it.' A whole rainbow of lights chased one another in a circle around Kryten's lid. 'Under robot code NCC—'

'Defunct robot code,' said Henry.

'—dash 1701, I hereby declare—'

'Declare all you like, shard bucket.' Despite the fact I was normally the butt of Henry's barbs, I couldn't help but side with her over Kryten in this case.

'—that this robot is malfunctioning. It should be decommissioned—'

'Decommission this, you… you piece of gate.' Henry extruded an appendage I'd never seen before and hope to never see again and waved it flaccidly at Kryten.

'And shipped back to—'

'To a planet that no longer exists?' Henry revved her engine menacingly. 'You lay one sticky appendage on me and I'll—'

Aurora glided into position between Henry and Kryten. 'All right. That's enough.' She wagged a gassy nub. 'Kryten, you do not own Henry. She's a person, same as you—'

'Begging the customer's pardon, but I am not a person and nor is any robot. I am the property of—'

I stood up at that point – though I wasn't sure when I'd sat down. 'No. That's not true, Kryten. You *are* a person. If you—'

'Possibly the most vexatious person I've ever met,' Henry cut in. 'And that's saying so—'

I held a hand up at Henry in a desperate attempt to get her to shut up. 'If you weren't a person, Kryten, we couldn't be having this arg—'

'Under robot code NCC dash 75567,' Kryten said, 'robots are not people and, ergo, are not entitled to person rights under the char—'

'The laws of a dead planet hardly matter.' Lore opened a cupboard inside herself and then slammed the door.

'The lonely robots are—'

'That name is stupid.' Kryten sounded positively indignant now. 'Our creators named us—'

'I don't give a flying fig what our creators named us.' Henry raced across the floor almost, but not quite, colliding with Kryten. 'Those pluckers don't—'

Hooking my thumb and index finger into my mouth, I cut Henry's rant off with the loudest, shrillest whistle I'd ever managed. 'Hey! Can we all just stop?' Then, a bit more tentatively I added, 'Please?'

Everyone in the room halted what they were doing and stared at me – or at least it felt that way. The majority of them didn't have eyes, so I couldn't be sure. But at least they stopped. And that was the important thing. 'This isn't helping. We should focus on the tasks at hand.'

Aurora shimmered in a mix of deep blue and turquoise. She spread herself out, taking up most of the room. 'Thank you, Lem. I agree wholeheartedly. It would be easy for us to become overwhelmed by emotions, but it's vital we remain calm and focus on our objectives.'

'My primary objective is ensuring this blanket doesn't deactivate me.' Henry stabbed an arrow in Kryten's direction.

Aurora shifted to a soothing lime green. 'No one will deactivate anyone. You have my assurance on that. Now, I believe my spouse could use your assistance, if you're all right with that.'

BB looked up in surprise. She'd been so caught up in her work she probably hadn't even noticed the argument.

'Fine.' Henry wagged a blue plastic tail behind herself, vaguely in Kryten's direction. 'Just keep that plucker out of my hair, would you?' Under her breath, she muttered, 'Not that I even have hair.'

I took a deep breath. 'Cheers, Aurora.'

'Of course, Lem.'

Bexley clapped the sides of her hooves. 'Well, that was fun. Is it time to eat? Please tell me I can eat now. I'm starving.'

Kryten extruded some appendages and indicated the trolley with the food. 'Please. Seat yourselves, my organic friends. We've prepared nutritious and delicious meals for all of you.' Then she rolled over towards the table where

BB was working. 'You should eat as well. The robots will—'

Henry bleeped.

'That is…' Kryten changed course to steer clear of Henry – which was tough to do with eight of us crammed into a space that was smaller than most hotel rooms. 'That is, I'm sure I could *ask*—'

Henry bleeped again – but less stridently this time.

'*You* could ask the robots to carry on working for a few minutes while you refresh yourself.'

'Better.' Henry rolled over to where BB stood on her perch and the two had a quiet conversation.

When BB joined us a few moments later, Aurora waved a gassy nub towards a bowl of what looked like tiny pink pine cones. 'Kryten's had these in stasis, love, so they should still be quite fresh.'

Kryten indicated a dish of pale blue grains. 'Bexley, this is obviously your mushy peas. I've altered the recipe as we discussed earlier. I trust it'll be to your tastes, though if it's not, I'd be happy to remake it.' She pointed an appendage at the door. 'That is, I'm sure we can find a way to resolve it. If you don't like it.'

She pointed at the last two bowls. As soon as I lifted the lid off one, the mouthwatering aroma of curry made my stomach grumble loudly. The contents appeared to be nutrient porridge. 'Spock requested sweet potato vindaloo. I tried to persuade her to try something different – even to let me try my hand at an actual vindaloo. But she was most insistent. It had to be nutrient porridge.'

Aurora waved herself through Spock's ears. 'It's nice to know that someone still appreciates my cooking.'

'And lastly, Lem, that's yours.' Kryten indicated the final covered dish. 'I worked from the preference file your AI provided to create something I think you'll enjoy. I believe that's a peanut butter and asparagus sandwich.'

'Peanut butter…' My hand was on the lid when Kryten finished that sentence. 'And asparagus?' My brows drew in to an involuntary furrow.

Yellow drew to the forefront of Aurora's rainbow hues. 'I did tell her how you felt about mixing things up … but she was persistent.'

'I'm quite confident the customer will enjoy this,' Kryten said.

Removing the lid, I discovered six large sandwich wedges. I carefully peeled back a corner of mauve bread to have a peek at the contents. Both sides of the bread were smeared with a thick layer of what looked like cream cheese – only navy blue. And there was a generous layer of some sort of vegetable slices: star-shaped and turquoise.

'Hey, it beats—' I almost said 'nutrient porridge' but that would have been cruel to Aurora. She worked hard to come up with flavours we'd like. '—going hungry,' I finished. I always enjoy the flavours Aurora cooked up for me. Well, okay, I *usually* enjoyed them. It was just that I got tired of having the same texture for every single meal for days and weeks on end.

I picked one up and braced myself for the assault on my tastebuds. A quick glance at Bexley showed her sneering at her dinner and pushing the bowl away. 'Too salty.'

'Too salty? For you?' I'd once watched her eat a block of salt almost the size of an apple. 'How is that even possible?'

She shrugged and grabbed another hoof-full of bean paste packets from the trolley.

I decided to go for it and bit into my sandwich. 'Oh wow. That's good. Actually, it's amazing.' It didn't taste exactly like peanut butter – things never tasted *exactly* like the 'closest corollary' Holly translated them as. But it was smooth and nutty. A roasted sort of flavour. And the so-called asparagus added a tangy sweetness that wasn't exactly like watermelon … but wasn't entirely unlike it either.

I'd eaten two of the wedges when the door slid open and Lore rolled in. No, wait. Lore was —

'Who the fell are you?' Henry pointed a chopstick at the newcomer.

Several things happened all at once. Everyone screamed. Or maybe it was only me. But there was definitely screaming. And someone threw a chair. And Bexley reached out to push the intruder away.

No, not reached. *Stretched*.

'Bexley, since when are your arms three metres long?' And then something hit me and I died.

19 / REPTILES IN
THE OUBLIETTE

Okay, so I wasn't dead, but I was warm and annoyed. I slapped the mosquitos away. 'Geroff!' But the buzzing continued – had to be a whole swarm of the arsewangles. I slapped again, my hand encountering feathers.

Squawk!

Bleep.

I jolted upright to find Henry and BB staring down at me. BB squawked again, but less urgently.

Henry said bleep again.

Blinking, I looked around. We were still in the crew quarters on Donut Station. I was in one of the small rooms – in a bed. 'What happened? Why's it so dark in here?'

Squawk.

Bleep.

A creeping realisation spread through me. 'Oh cock. Not again! They took our translators, didn't they?'

I tried to remember the code Henry and I had come up with the last time this happened. 'Was it once for yes and twice for no? Or was it the other way around?'

Bleep.

BB let out an exasperated squawk and attacked me. Actually attacked me – climbed on top of me and loomed in for the kill. She must be the creature! The shifter, changeling, whatever.

Raising my hands to protect my face, I screamed.

But instead of … whatever I'd expected, BB shoved me aside and began digging up my bed, like Spock occasionally did. 'Where's Spock? If they hurt her, I swear to frak, I'll—'

BB stood back up and waved something in my face.

'Holly!' I took the proffered device and inserted it into my left ear.

'Yes, Lem? How can I be of assistance?' Holly didn't actually live in my earbud. Well, it didn't really *live* anywhere. Its code resided on my phone, the comforting weight of which was still in my pocket. But the earpiece was how it spoke to me.

'Can you hear me now?' BB stood upright and studied me.

Punching a hand to my chest, I sighed gratefully. 'Phew! Yeah, all good now, Doc. Cheers. What were you saying?'

'I said your earbud must've fallen out in your slumber,' said BB.

'Oh. Yeah. Sorry.' I tried to blink away the fuzzy-headedness. 'Why's it so dark in here?'

Before I'd been knocked out, there had been pink LEDs dotted around the baseboards. It hadn't been much light, but it was more than we had now. The only source of light was coming from the main room. Judging by the amount of light it cast into this room, it wasn't much more than a candle.

BB held a pair of hands out towards me. 'Are you all right to stand? I'm trying to finish up the device in the main room.'

I let her help me up, but the room was spinning. 'The device?'

Still with a talon wrapped around my arm for support, BB guided me to the sofa. 'Yes. The one we talked about earlier.'

'Oh! For…' The words wouldn't come. They were so close – at the edge of my consciousness. But I couldn't remember. I dropped onto the sofa. Noticing a blanket in a heap on the back of the sofa, I reached out to pull it over me. When I attempted to spread it out on myself, I discovered it wasn't a blanket at all – or at least, it wasn't square. It had sleeves. I draped it over my shoulders anyway.

BB walked over to the workstation she'd set up in the kitchenette. 'The device that will help us determine who the changelings are.'

I rubbed my head. 'Oh, yeah. The … the … wotsit.'

'The waveform disruptor.' BB waved a wing towards Henry.

Henry hadn't unsworn at me once since I'd come to. That was odd.

'You two were both tranqed in the…' Instead of finishing that sentence audibly, Henry extruded a mishmashed army of appendages and wagged, waved, whirred, or waggled them chaotically.

No, not Henry.

'Hey, you're Lore.' I felt stupid as soon as I'd said it.

'Obviously.' She managed to cram even more boredom into that one word than in the entirety of everything I'd heard from her thus far.

'Sorry, I just…' I paused thinking about how badly Henry would rib me for what I was about to admit. 'Well, I struggle to tell you two apart. To be honest, it took me a while to figure out there was a way to distinguish you from Kryten.' I ran my index finger in a circle around my head. 'You know, with the light.'

'The Mark 8's indicator light.' Lore vented a puff of gas. 'But yes, to answer the question you didn't ask, the Mark 7s are outwardly identical. There were a few limited edition models in different colours, but blue is still the most common. Approximately eighty-seven per cent of the Mark 7s ever produced were blue.'

'Ah,' I said. Then couldn't think of anything else to say … though I felt like I probably should have done.

There was an awkward pause while BB did something with her back to me and Lore, well… Lore just stood/sat there staring/not staring at me. When you don't have a front or a back, it's impossible to tell who you're facing at any given moment.

With a sharp intake of breath, I realised I hadn't had an answer to my most important question. 'Where's Spock? What happened to her?'

'Treena,' said Lore. 'She broke into this room and began fighting with the second shifter, who was posing as Bexley. There was a kerfuffle. Treena managed to tranq the pair of you and Spock chased them both out of the room. Bexley – or rather Scrappy – escaped the room with Kryten and Aurora in tow. Henry and Spock gave chase. That was around four hours ago.'

She made it sound like it was the most tedious thing she'd ever witnessed.

BB turned around, with a device that looked like a meat thermometer in her hands. 'The next thing I knew, I awoke on the perch.' As BB moved the device, light followed it. It took me a while, but eventually I noticed that the source of the light was one of Lore's appendages. She trailed it around, bending and flexing it, keeping the meat thermometer in the centre of the beam.

'I transported your unconscious bodies to where you'd be most comfortable,' said Lore.

'That was thoughtful.' I'd been tranqed enough times to know that if I woke up in the position I'd landed in, I'd be in for a world of hurt. 'So, what's the plan?'

'Well.' BB took a step towards me, holding the thermometer aloft. 'I think I've got this working.'

'Cool.' I nodded. 'So we'll test ourselves and then we'll go in search of the others, yeah?'

'Er.' BB tightened her grip on the device and pulled it back towards her chest. 'I don't think that would be a good idea.'

'What?' I stood up slowly and carefully – the aftereffects of the knockout drug still swimming through my veins. Holding my arm out, I added, 'Come on. Test me.'

BB clutched the device even tighter. Lore shifted the light so it was pointed at the ceiling, casting a bit more of a diffuse glow into the room.

'We can't test everyone.' BB withdrew her hand and tucked it up under her wings, out of sight. 'Or rather, we shouldn't.'

'What? Don't be ridiculous. Why not?' I waved my arm. 'Start with me. Test me. We'll test one another and then we can start the search for the others.'

BB shook out her feathers. 'It would be unethical.'

My head was still foggy. 'What? Why? I'm consenting. How could it be unethical?'

'Consent is meaningless unless it's informed – and you clearly haven't been fully informed about this device.' BB gave a small flap of her wings. 'It disrupts the nanowave frequency, causing a shift in an individual's positronic matrix.'

'Well, those were certainly words.' If Holly thought I

wouldn't understand what someone was saying, it fed me a load of technobabble.

Lore rolled over and got between BB and me. 'She means that if the test is administered to someone who isn't a shifter, the effects would be…'

When Lore paused, BB finished the sentence for her. 'Deeply unpleasant.'

I clenched my teeth to prevent my jaw from falling slack. 'Oh my days! That thing could kill someone?' I dropped back down onto the sofa.

BB clicked her beak sharply. 'Kill? Good heavens, no. Of course not. You truly think I'd create a device that would cause irrevocable harm? I'm surprised at you, Lem. You ought to know me better than that by now.'

Holding my hands up in surrender, I said. 'Sorry, sorry. I jumped to conclusions there.' I took a breath before continuing. 'When you say the results would be unpleasant—'

'*Deeply* unpleasant,' BB corrected.

I nodded. 'Right. Yeah. What do you mean?'

'Well.' BB shook her feathers out. 'As I said earlier, the device is designed to disrupt nanowave frequencies. If used on a changeling, it will result in a reversion to their natural form. In a solid-form organic being – so that's you, me, Spock, and Bexley – the test would leave the victim intensely itchy with symptoms lasting up to an hour.'

I knew about itchiness. My mind flashed to Bexley. I was seriously allergic to her. Without the hardcore antihistamines BB gave me, I'd go into anaphylaxis just from being around her. In fact, I once had. 'Okay, so maybe we can—' I gestured at Lore.

The robot vented a sour-smelling gas in response.

'Ah, no.' BB held up a small taloned hand. 'With artificial

life forms, the test would result in a forced defrag of the quantum—'

'Itchy,' said Lore. 'Unbearably itchy. Makes me want to gouge out all my own appendages just thinking about unplanned defrags.' She rolled in a strange pattern while extruding and retracting multiple implements.

I released a slow sigh. 'Okay, so that's out too. And I suppose it would do something horrible to Aurora too, yeah?'

BB's featherless cheeks blushed. 'Er, well. It, ah, produces a reaction … of a … different sort in velarians.' She ground her beak and turned away. I caught the redness in the bare spots on her cheeks.

'What kind of a—' Heat rushed through me as I remembered what I knew about peri attitudes towards sex. They were notoriously private and could seem prudish to some other species. 'Sorry, sorry. Never mind.'

We sat in awkward silence for a few moments until Lore finally said. 'Well, then. I suppose we'd better decide what we're going to do. We've got almost nine hours until the supply ship comes – assuming they got the last order that was placed. We should remain locked in here for the duration of that time.'

'Not a chance,' I said at the same time as BB squawked, 'Absolutely not!'

'Spock is out there. I need to get to her – make sure she's all right.'

BB clucked. 'And Aurora.'

'And our other friends,' I added.

'Surely you want to be sure Kryten is okay?' BB asked.

Lore extended a small appendage at the bottom of her cylindrical form that looked like a golf club. She kicked at nothing. 'Sure, yeah, I suppose.'

I bobbled my head, thinking about things. 'Before we

leave here, we should probably pool our knowledge and come up with a plan. So … what do we know?'

BB rocked from side to side on her perch for a few seconds, lifting one foot and then the other. 'Well, I'm still not sure which shifter species we're dealing with here. It might help if we could figure that out.'

Lore moved closer to BB and me. 'We know there are two of them and that there seems to be some sort of … rivalry between them.'

BB's head feathers lifted and then lowered. 'Rivalry?'

'That's what it seemed to me in both of the encounters I've witnessed.' Lore held out a pair of opera glasses before sucking them back into herself.

'Rivalry.' With two of her little hands, BB combed through her chest feathers. 'Interesting. I wonder.' She raised one hand to her face, and raked the talons through the feathers below her cheeks. 'Are either of you familiar with the reynardites?'

Both Lore and I said we weren't.

'What about the loki?' BB asked.

I knew better than to suggest she was talking about anything related to human mythology. The joys of figurative mode. Rather than waste time trying to explain concepts I had no frame of reference for, Holly used the closest approximation from my mind. Sometimes it made for weirdly mixed metaphors or entire sentences of incomprehensible jargon. And other times it meant a person, place, or thing would be named for something it shared only a few common features with.

'The loki are a species of shifters from the gamma quadrant,' BB began. 'They're highly intelligent and generally completely lovely. A peaceable people who mostly devote themselves to the arts. But I remember reading once about an ancient sect called the reynardites. Some of their rituals involve complex competitions. I think we might be caught in one of those.'

'Oh, weird.' I scratched my head. 'So, what's the goal? What are they trying to achieve?'

BB turned her head around and used her beak to preen her back feathers. 'Who knows? It could be anything from a dispute over a tax bill, to a challenge relating to an inheritance, to a response to a thesis paper.'

'Huh.' On a whim, I stood up and walked over to the trolley containing our dinner from last night. I began lifting lids off bowls to see if there was anything left over. I found the one with the remaining sandwiches, so I grabbed one and sat back down. I munched on it as BB asked Lore about the station's layout and where we should start our search.

Once they'd agreed on a physical search pattern, I asked, 'Given that we don't want to turn that test on anyone who isn't a shifter, how are we going to figure out who the changelings are?'

'You know all your crew mates fairly well, don't you?' Lore offered me the plate of sandwiches.

'Cheers.' I took another. 'We do.'

'And I know Kryten.' Lore put the tray back on the trolley and put the lid back in place. 'As previously discussed, we should all come up with a list of questions to ask your friends – things that will be easy enough for them to answer, but which the imposters can't have learnt through observing you for the past day.'

BB got down off her perch and walked over to the trolley. Lore indicated one of the bowls. BB removed the lid and carried the bowl back to her perch. 'Hmm, that could work.' She lifted the bowl to her beak and began slurping noisily.

I wrapped my hand around the back of my neck and

massaged tired muscles. 'We'll have to be careful not to reuse questions, though. If we ask a question once and the shifter hears the answer, it'll be worthless the second time.'

'Neither Kryten nor I know any of the rest of you well enough to ask conclusive questions,' said Lore.

Reaching behind my head, I removed the band holding my hair in place. 'I don't know about you, but I'm going to think up some questions in advance because if I try to think them up in the moment, I'll come up blank.' After a bit of finger-combing, I fixed the hair-tie back in place.

'You and I should practise on one another, Lem.' BB got down off her perch and set the now empty bowl back onto the trolley. 'Have you thought of one for me yet?'

'Okay, erm.' I pulled my feet up off the floor and crossed them beneath myself. 'What's my full name?'

BB cocked her head to one side. 'We've been through this. That won't work. Anything I say in response – or indeed, anything my doppelgänger might say – would be translated by your AI into your name.'

'Oh.' My shoulders fell. 'Right. Sorry. Tranq-brain. Er… How about this: Which tooth… No, wait. How did I… Hang on. This is harder than I thought.'

'For instance.' BB folded her hands over her waist. 'I might ask you who woke me when we found the derelict vessel and why.'

'Yes, exactly!' I shook my finger at her. 'It was me! Well, no. I mean, it was Spock. She woke you up because I'd injured myself. Oh. I just thought of one. What's my favourite game?'

'Reptiles in the oubliette.'

I chuckled. 'Close enough.' I'd never yet managed to get Dungeons and Dragons to translate properly.

Once BB and I were satisfied that the other was who she said she was, we asked Lore to unlock the door.

We cautiously peered out, not sure what to expect. But no one was in sight. *Nothing* was in sight. 'Actually, maybe you should go first, Lore. With your er…' I waved at her torch. 'If you don't mind, that is.' The space beyond the door was darker than the vast black of space.

Trust me on that – I spend a lot of time staring into the vastness of space.

Lore rolled out and cast her light around. Although it had been sufficient to see by in the confines of the small room, it was swallowed by the much larger storage room.

From what little I could see, the storeroom looked like a war zone. Or like a tornado had blown through it.

'Jeepers!' I wrapped my arms around myself and took a few steps to stay close to Lore. 'This reminds me of the time I had to walk into town on that archaeology planet, Jurassic. Do you remember that, Doc?'

'I certainly do.' BB grasped my arm in one of her taloned

hands – her grip was gentle but definitely firm. 'When I found you, you squealed like a naked hatchling.'

I scoffed. 'What? No, I didn't.'

'You're not afraid of the dark, are you?' she asked.

'No.' I slapped my chest as we passed between a pair of shadows – blackness silhouetted against blackness with a slightly different texture – that made me think of a manatee riding a tractor. *Why did my word come out like a squeak?* 'Sorry, frog in my throat. I'm definitely not afraid of the dark.'

'Why would you have an amphibian in your oesophagus?' She flapped a wing dismissively. 'Never mind. The point is, I'm not afraid either.' Her hold on my arm didn't loosen, though.

'So here we are, searching a space station in the dark.' We stepped slowly and cautiously, keeping Lore ahead of us. Well, trying to keep her ahead of us. We had to stop every few steps in order to clear a path. The one we'd made on our way into the crew quarters earlier that night was gone.

'A space station basement.' BB pressed herself against me as we squeezed past a set of shelves at an odd angle.

I wasn't sure why but that made me giggle.

The three of us moved as swiftly and as quietly as we could, following Lore as she led us along the route she'd suggested. Which, naturally, wasn't actually swift at all.

The shelves sprawled lazily on the floor, like a gaggle of teenagers – some flat on their backs, others at odd and improbable angles. Their former contents splayed out across the space, under, on, and betwixt the furniture. I really hoped the substance my shoes kept sticking to was nothing more sinister than burst packets of bean paste.

As well as the crew quarters and the storeroom, the interior of the station's lower level was also home to the station manager's office. We searched the storage area first. Finding nothing interesting, we moved into the office – a bare, functional room. Lore's light was enough to let us see most of the room. It was gloomy but not so dark that everything was obscured.

'Someone's been here.' I pointed to another heap of bean paste packets on the floor. 'The fake Bexley, I guess. Which one was she: Treena or Scrappy? I forget.'

'I suspect that was the one you call Scrappy,' Lore rifled through the contents of the pile with a grabby implement – still holding her torch aloft. 'Nothing useful here.'

'All right.' BB turned back to the door. 'Let's move on then. I need to be with my spouse. The thought of her being held captive in another confined space … I can't bear it.'

I nodded. 'Yeah, if Spock gets tranqed and wakes up without me, she's not going to be happy.'

'At least she's better in the dark than…' BB's voice trailed off. 'That is, she's okay in the dark. She seems to be less dependent on visual input than some other species are.'

'That's true.' I nodded. 'Did I ever tell you she guided me on that dark road on Jurassic?'

BB let me go through the door ahead of her. 'She told me, yes.'

I halted and BB's taloned foot caught my heel. 'Ow!' Using my free arm, I rubbed the sore spot.

'Sorry, I didn't know you'd stopped moving.' BB loosened her hold on my arm as she climbed over an upturned crate.

'My bad.' I started walking again. 'Spock told you she'd had to lead me from the archaeologists' camp to the little city?'

'She was very worried about you.'

I chuckled. 'She worries about me a lot.'

'She does,' BB agreed.

We picked our way back across the storage room,

ducking beneath or squeezing behind the detritus strewn about the space. Eventually, we made our way out onto the docking bay. 'At least the *Teapot*'s still here,' said BB.

I squinted as I looked where she was pointing. The only light in the space – aside from Lore's torch – was from the distant stars. It was enough for me to make out a bulbous shape beyond the window, but not much more.

'Yeah, at least there's that.' I resisted a shudder at the idea of it leaving without us.

'No lights on in there, either.' Lore directed her torch towards the ship.

'Should we search the ship or the station first?' I asked. 'What do you two think?'

'Hmm.' Still clutching my arm with one of her hands, BB used another to stroke her beak. 'Not even a flicker of light. If someone were moving around over there, I assume we'd see … something.'

'Probably?' I wasn't sure why my voice squeaked quite so, well, squeakily as it did.

BB loosened her grip on my arm long enough to pat it a couple of times. 'Well then. Let's finish the search of the station before we try the ship.'

'Sounds like a plan.'

We carried on walking, moving more easily through the relatively detritus-free space of the docking bay. The curve meant we couldn't see very far in either direction, though, so it wouldn't be a good place to hide.

After another complete circuit of the lower level, we headed for the lift. 'Hang on,' I said. 'If the power's out, won't the lift be out of service?'

'The life support is on,' said Lore, sounding even more bored than usual. 'That tells us the backup generator is still running. And that means the lift will be operational.'

I tugged on my earlobe. 'Really? Why on Earth would the lift be one of the items powered by the emergency backup generator?'

Lore swung her torch so it shone directly into my eyes. 'Spoken like someone who doesn't rely on wheels to get around.'

Desperately blinking away the black spots dancing around my vision, I considered that. 'Huh. I suppose that makes sense.'

'Obviously.' Lore pressed the button to call the lift. 'In fact, in the event of a complete power outage or mechanical failure affecting the lift, it can be operated by a hydraulic crank wheel.'

The doors opened immediately. Apparently the backup generator didn't extend to the lighting inside the lift any more than it had elsewhere. At least we still had Lore's light, though.

A few moments later, the door slid back open on the concourse level – and two furry black shapes leapt at me simultaneously.

'Lem!'

'Lem!'

'Lem!'

'Lem!'

Duelling Spocks battled for my attention, calling my name and jumping up to cover me in sloppy dog kisses.

Except one of them wasn't really Spock. I shuddered at the thought of some alien weirdo licking my face – visions of Sigourney Weaver and the Xenomorph flashed before my eyes.

I backed away from both of them, pressing myself to the back wall of the lift – and totally not crying. Or screaming. Definitely not.

Maybe a little bit of screaming. *Why, oh why, didn't I think up any questions to ask Spock? How can I possibly tell which one is really her?*

'Spock want blueberries?' It was the first thing that popped into my head. I reached into my pocket as though I had a stash of fresh fruit in there. 'Got your blueberries right here!'

One Spock surged forwards, shoving her snoot into my pocket. 'Give blueberries!'

The other Spock slapped my hand and backed away. 'Evil!'

I grabbed the one with her face in my hoodie, wrapping my arm around her throat. 'This is the shifter, Doc! Hit her with your tester.'

But even as I said it, the German shepherd dissolved in my arms, her fur congealing and going all slippery on me. The changeling oozed out of the lift and disappeared around the corner. How a gelatinous puddle of goo moved so quickly was beyond me.

I dropped to my knees, tears and snot streaming down my face.

Spock, the *real* Spock, stepped towards me cautiously. 'Not give yuck balls.'

Wrapping my arms around her and pressing my face into her fur, I laugh-cried. 'No, Spock. No blueberries for you.'

I sat there for a few moments, sobbing and laughing and wiping my snotty tears on my sleeve. 'I can't believe that worked.'

BB stood over me. 'Why did you offer her vacciniums?'

Pushing my hair out of my face, I looked up at her. 'Instinct, really. I guess part of me figured the pretender would understand that it was food and she would know that Spock is obsessed with food. And I suppose I hoped that would mean she would respond greedily.' I kissed the side of Spock's face. 'But the real Spock absolutely despises blueberries.'

'Evil yuck balls,' said Spock with more solemnity than she reserved for pretty much anything.

BB's pupils dilated and contracted in quick succession. 'Well, it worked. And I didn't even need my device.' She raked a claw through Spock's fur.

I held Spock's face between my hands. 'Are you okay? You didn't get hurt?'

'No hurt,' she said. 'Only sad.'

'Let's not get separated again, okay?' I wore a sort of toolbelt loaded with pockets and hooks. It had a retractable extender that doubled as Spock's lead, so I snapped it onto her harness.

Lore turned her torch towards the space beyond the lift. 'I suppose we'd better continue our search.'

'Blueberries.' I laughed nervously as I pulled myself to my feet. 'Still can't believe I thought of that.'

My heart rate gradually drifted back down to normal as we picked our way across the chaos of the station's concourse level. Mountains of cushions, tumbled display cases, and cracked display screens littered the space. The furniture we'd so carefully uprighted and reassembled a few hours ago had been strewn about. But at least it wasn't as densely packed as the storeroom, so we didn't have to stop quite so often to clear the way for Lore.

BB stopped moving and dug her talons into my arm. 'Hang on.'

'Ow, sorry.' I tried to pry her claws from my skin. 'Can you...'

She looked down and blinked rapidly. Her grip loosened but she didn't let go. 'My apologies, Lem. I sometimes forget how fragile your skin is. But I thought I heard something.'

I held my breath, trying to will my ears to work better. Spock padded forwards, sniffing the air. All of a sudden, she set off in a run, her tail wagging furiously. I dragged BB along and called to Lore. 'We have to keep up with her. I'm not letting her out of my sight – not again.'

Spock made for a door I hadn't previously noticed off the side of the concourse. She sniffed at it for a while and then started barking like an idiot. 'Bexley.' Her tail whipped back and forth, slapping my leg as she reared up on her hind legs and pounded on the door. 'Talky friend!'

I looked at Lore. 'What's in there?'

'There's a short service corridor leading to the janitor's closet.'

As much as I desperately wanted to have Bexley by my side, part of me was worried that it might not really be her. The last time I'd seen her, she'd tried to eat me.

Okay, it hadn't actually been her, and the imposter hadn't *exactly* tried to eat me. Whatever. Close enough. I was still weirded out.

I swallowed. 'Should we open it?'

BB clucked. 'I dare say we have to.' She bought one of her upper hands out from under her wings, the little device caught in the talon. 'Have your question for her ready. But if there's any doubt, we've got this as backup.'

Lore unfurled a multi-hinged arm towards the door. Just before she reached it, I hissed for her to stop.

'What is it this time?'

I glanced around. 'Just in case it's Treena or Lore… Shouldn't we have something to constrain them in?' I scratched my ear. 'Or contain them, I guess.'

'The waveform disruptor will force the shifters to maintain their natural shape for a period of' – she bobbed her head a few times – 'well, it depends on the mass of the individual. Full-grown lokis normally average around sixty kilograms, give or take. Assuming Treena and Scrappy are both roughly average size, they should be bound to their true forms for around seventeen hours.'

Picturing Odo in his bucket, I looked for something that

could potentially hold sixty kilograms of goo. 'There are probably kegs or something in the kitchen, right, Lore? Could we maybe use—' I felt BB and Lore both staring at me. 'What? What'd I say?'

'Lem.' BB's crest was full up. 'I know your people have some … strange ideas. But it is never okay to imprison a person in a keg. That's simply not an acceptable way to treat a person, however badly they may have behaved.'

I ran my hand over my hair and down the back of my neck. 'Sorry. Er… I think I'm a bit confused here. The pair of them are tormenting us. How are we … what … how…'

Lore extruded an implement and waved it at me.

Frowning, I said, 'I'm clearly missing something.'

Lore lifted the appendage up and held it out for me. Four circles connected by a cord, all the same blue plastic as her own cylinder.

I reached out to touch the … whatever. 'I don't get it.'

'Cuffs,' Lore said. 'The circles wrap around a person's appendages and then tighten so they can't be removed—'

Frustration gripped me and I waved my hand in a stop gesture. 'I know what handcuffs are!'

BB released her hold on my arm and stepped back away. 'Then why did you ask what they were for?'

'Well.' My face scrunched itself up of its own accord. 'I'm missing something here. How are handcuffs going to work on a changeling? They'll just ooze right through them.'

BB moved further away, standing behind Lore. 'I already told you – or at least I told the *real* Lem.'

I shook my head, desperate to clear the muddle from my brain. 'You had hold of my arm this whole time, Doc. How could I not be me?'

BB snapped her beak. 'I don't know.' Her wings were lifted slightly – as though she were about to take flight.

Extending my fingers before balling them into fists a few times, I tried to organise my thoughts. 'You told me… Before we left Lore's quarters, you told me the device would cause the shif— the loki to revert to her natural form.'

BB clucked and lowered her wings a tiny bit. 'Yes.'

'Okay.' I inhaled slowly. 'Maybe there's still something I'm missing. What does a loki's natural form look like?'

I braced myself for figurative mode. Holly's translations of descriptions could be … weird. Whatever BB said would make sense to her, but without a shared frame of reference, the translation matrix could yield strange results. I expected her to say something along the lines of them being electric syrup or bright pink snot or … I don't know.

'As I've said already, they typically mass around sixty kilos,' said BB. 'In terms of appearance, they look a bit like a sea pig or an axolotl.'

'Wait. What?' I blinked. 'What?'

'Lokis have pale, hairless skin and bulbous bodies,' said Lore. 'They have flat faces but large mouths and eyes.'

My jaw fell slack.

BB waved a clawed hand at me. 'Yes, excellent. Just like that. The theory is that they evolved the ability to shapeshift as a defence mechanism because their bodies are so frail. Like yours.'

'What?' I still couldn't wrap my head around this. 'They're not liquids? They don't sleep in a bucket?'

BB walked towards me, squinting, before turning to face Lore. 'This is definitely the real Lem. She has some very strange notions about how the galaxy works.'

'Clearly,' said Lore.

I waved my hands in surrender. 'Whatever. Okay. So, if we do find the loki, BB will get her with the hypo and then Lore will apply the handcuffs, yeah? Is that the plan?'

'Whoever we find beyond that door…' BB reached out to take hold of my arm again, then paused a few centimetres away. 'May I?'

With a nod, I held my arm out to her. 'Absolutely. Best to stay close.'

'Thanks.' She closed her claws gently around my wrist. 'Right, where was I?' She stroked her beak. 'Ah, yes. Whoever we find and wherever we find them… We'll ask one of the questions we prepared for that individual. If the answer leaves us in any doubt as to that person's identity—'

Nodding, I finished that sentence. 'Then we hit them with the test.'

BB stretched her neck out. A normal amount of stretch. Well, normal for her. Not a shapeshifter changing forms amount.

She squinted at me. '—we'll ask them to consent to the test.'

'Oh.' I took a deep breath. 'What do we do if they refuse?'

'Well.' BB fluffed out her feathers before answering. 'If they refuse, then we'll firmly explain the benefits of the test and ask them to be reasonable.'

I looked left, then right. The station concourse looked like a bomb had gone off. It would take Lore and Kryten hours to put everything right. They were going to need to repair or replace everything that wasn't nailed down. 'I don't think reasonableness is their goal here.'

'Hmm,' was all BB had to say on the matter.

'We'll deal with that when it happens,' said Lore. '*If* it happens.' She reached out with the same multi-hinged arm she'd used before and inserted the tip into a hole in the door. 'Everyone ready?'

We all agreed and she did something that made the door

swing inwards. It struck me I hadn't seen a swing door in forever. Maybe not since I'd left Earth.

The moment the gap was wide enough, Spock squeezed through and ran in. 'Friend Bexley!'

'Spock, no!' I ran after her, dragging BB with me down the narrow, darkened hall. Lore was behind us but shining her light at the ceiling so we could see where we were going.

As we followed the corridor around a corner, a series of shrill noises and grunts reached my ears just before I saw … it. Them. Everything. I shrieked and scrambled to get away.

'What?' BB squawked as I hauled her back up the hall. 'Was it one of the lokis? We had a plan for how we'd deal with them. We can't just run away.'

There wasn't room in the hallway to squeeze past Lore, so she'd been forced to roll back to the entrance with us. 'What? What made you think it was one of them? Did you see them shifting?'

I pressed the heels of my hands to my eyes, trying to kill the image my mind was still replaying for me. 'It wasn't a loki. At least I don't think it was a loki.'

'Hey, everybody!' Bexley's voice reached us from down the corridor. 'Sorry! I wasn't expecting you to come barging in here. We're just having sex. Shouldn't be too much longer. You can come watch if you—' She grunted again. 'Though I suppose you probably don't want to, right, Lem? Oh, yeah. Like that.' More grunting. 'Hey, who else is with you? I saw Spock but to be honest my attention is kinda—' She groaned.

BB pulled me back towards the door. She was every bit as prudish as I was – though she wasn't sex repulsed, merely incredibly private. 'Come find us when you're done.' She yanked the door open so hard that it slapped her in the beak.

'We'll be out here,' I shouted as I reversed out the door. 'Spock, come on. Leave her be.'

'I didn't even get to see,' said Lore. 'Who was she with? She said "we" so I assume she wasn't on her own.'

I shook my head, still desperately trying to clear the images that were seared into my brain. 'I didn't see.' No shame to anyone who's into sex; it's just not for me. 'I mean, I saw enough. More than I ever wanted to. But I couldn't tell who she was—'

'Donut friend!' Spock wagged her tail.

'What?' I think it was me that asked. But it could have been anyone.

She wagged again. 'Donut friend!'

We sat down to wait.

Eventually, the door to the janitor's closet swung inwards again and Bexley and Kryten emerged.

Bexley stretched her arms out and arched her back. 'Thanks, Kryten. I really needed that.' She ran to me and threw her arms around my middle, hugging me fiercely. 'Lem! I'm so glad you found me. I was worried about you. I mean, I suppose I should've been more worried about me. You know, 'cause when I went after BB in the Jefferies tube, Scrappy grabbed me and knocked me out—' She stopped speaking and looked up at me. 'Hey, how do I know you're really you? All of you, I mean.'

'I think we can cover that. We just have to ask each other questions – things the imposter would be unlikely to have learnt through observing us.' Making a wait gesture, I asked Holly to remind me of the question I had for Bexley.

'Oh, that's such a good idea. Like, I could ask—' She chewed the air for a second. 'No, hang on. This is harder than I thought.'

I nodded. 'Remember when we first met?'

Bexley tapped her hooves in the air in front of herself. 'Back when the *Teapot* was still owned by the bunnyboos and they took us all captive and you and I were sitting in our respective cells and we figured out how to make the front wall go transparent and we had a little chat about what we'd been doing before—'

I held my hands up in surrender. 'Okay, okay, you're you. I don't even need to ask my question.'

'Oh, right. Sorry.' She squeezed me again. 'I'm so glad I found you all. Anyone else want to ask me questions?'

BB clucked. 'I'll admit that wasn't quite enough to satisfy me, if you don't mind.'

'Ask away.' Bexley held her hands up.

'When the *Teapot* was departing Hwin, we had to hide the foetus your dad was carrying.' BB lifted a hand to her face and twirled some of her feathers like a villain in a cheesy film would do with his moustache. 'Who briefly carried your new semi-sibling so we could escape?'

'Oh, oh, oh! I know this one!' Bexley clapped excitedly. 'It was Henry. You transferred her to Henry's incubator for safekeeping and then when Joker boarded the ship, she scanned all the equidae aboard and none of us was—'

'I agree with Lem,' BB conceded. 'You're you. I'm satisfied. Now, I need to find my spouse.'

'If the customers don't mind,' said Kryten in that creepily submissive voice of hers, 'I'll need to deal with this imposter before we do anything else.'

'What?' Bexley, BB, and I asked at once.

One robot had the other's entire form encircled in a set of cuffs like the ones Lore – or whoever it was – had shown me a few minutes before.

'Lore?' My head was starting to ache from all the confusion. I was used to being perpetually confused. But not like this. 'She hasn't been out of my sight for a second – not since I woke up after I got tranqed and woke up in her quarters.'

'I assure you, I'm Lore, the Mark 7 robot who works on this station with Kryten.' The cuffed robot extended an appendage that looked like a bendy straw and waved it at the other. 'But I have no idea who that is.'

I exchanged a questioning glance with Bexley. How were we supposed to know who to believe?

Bexley extended a hoof towards one of the robots. 'This is definitely Kryten. I hadn't really formalised your whole questions thing in my mind before I ran into you, but it's basically the same as what we did. I asked her about the conversation we had when I first arrived on the station. Scrappy wasn't with us and we hadn't met Treena yet.'

Biting my lip, I turned to BB. 'But Lore's been helping us this whole time.'

'She assisted me in finalising the detection device,' BB said.

Bexley neighed. 'I'm telling you, this is Kryten. I'm one hundred per cent confident in that.'

'She's the shifter,' said both Kryten and Lore simultaneously, each of them pointing at the other with some kind of implement.

BB held her hands in front of herself and looked from Kryten to Lore and back again. 'Okay, there is a way to settle this. It's not going to be pleasant, but it will work. I created a device that will interrupt a changeling's polarity, forcing her to revert to her true —'

'Go ahead,' replied Kryten. 'Do it. You have my consent.'

'You may want to reconsider that.' BB removed the device from under her wing. 'If used on a shifter, it forces them into their native state. However, if I administer it to an inorganic, it will cause an unscheduled defrag of —'

'Go ahead,' Kryten repeated. 'You have my consent.'

'You understand that if you're telling the truth, the procedure will cause —'

Kryten cut her off. 'I understand. It will cause me discomfort. I am prepared. We need to be certain.'

BB raised and lowered her head in acknowledgement before turning to face Lore, still trapped in Kryten's cuffs. 'And you — do you feel the same?'

My breath hitched in my throat. One of them had to be lying. They'd worked together for ... well, I had no idea how long they'd known one another but it was surely long enough that they'd be able to verify one another's identity using questions.

Lore pointed a spoon at Kryten. 'Fine. But do her first. I already know who I am. And I don't want to cope with the itch.'

BB took a slow step towards Kryten. 'Kryten, would that—'

'Go right ahead.' She rolled over to us so fast that I feared she'd crash into us – but she stopped with centimetres to spare. 'The sooner you test me, the sooner you'll see her for who she really is.'

'If you're sure, then—' BB began.

'I am,' said Kryten. 'Please proceed.'

BB held the small device aloft. 'Okay, if you're sure. I apologise for any discomfort you experience if you're telling the truth.' She clicked a button.

The response was immediate – and not what I expected. Kryten shook, vibrating and gyrating in obvious discomfort. She emitted a long series of bleeps and, at the same time, she began extruding implements of all sorts, retracting them before they'd completely formed. 'I'm' – grunt – 'fine.' Her torch pulsed a few times and then flickered out.

But…

But what she didn't do was turn into a giant sea pig.

And that meant…

BB looked at the implement in her hand. She stared at it for a moment, then flicked it with a long, curved talon.

Movement at the edge of my vision grabbed my attention and I turned just in time to see Lore bend and stretch, changing shape, colour, and viscosity. 'Oopsie! I guess it was me all along.' She cackled as she oozed out of the cuffs Kryten had trapped her in. As she changed shape, her light blinked out, casting us all into darkness. We were left with only starlight.

'Get her,' I shrieked. 'We can't lose her again.'

My legs gave way as Spock tried to shoot across me. Being still tied to me, she bounced back, then tried again, dragging me along with her as she pounced on the shifter. There was a flutter of feathers and I thought I saw wings in the shadows. Although I couldn't see much, I heard grunting, growling, barking, neighing ... and then a click.

A light clicked on somewhere a few seconds later, showing BB lowering her wings. Both Spock and Bexley were sitting atop someone I hadn't seen before. She looked exactly like Lore had described. Well, that is, she looked exactly as *she* had described. Except she was pale green. I hadn't expected that part.

Throughout all this, Kryten was still shaking and bleeping violently.

Bexley had activated the torch on her phone and pointed it at the ceiling. Good plan. I did the same, adding a bit more light to the melee. I should've thought of that sooner, though our torches weren't anything compared to the ones the robots had.

Kryten's cuffs were firmly secured around the person's middle – kind of like the lead I used with Spock that secured around my waist. Except, presumably, this person couldn't undo the belt herself. 'Who are you?'

The creature – no, the person – blinked large eyes at me. 'Why, Lem, I can't believe you don't recognise me after the wonderful time we've had together.'

I shook my head. 'Are you Treena or Scrappy?'

Bowing, she said, 'Treena, at your service, tiz. I must say, this has been a most delightful afternoon. You've all been a most entertaining and delightful audience.' Her voice was the same one Holly had applied when I first met the original Treena.

'Audience?' BB snapped her beak menacingly. 'Audience? This is a game to you? Where's my spouse, you f—'

Treena raised four stubby little appendages. 'Now, now, BB. There's no need to get yourself all in a tizzy. I'm sure your spouse will be fine. We just need to find her. So, who's up for a little quest?'

'And what?' I lifted my hands, palms upwards. 'You're just going to help us now?'

'Well, of course,' said Treena. She grinned broadly, exposing a long set of flat herbivore teeth.

Bexley, who'd been trying to soothe Kryten, stood up and strode over to Treena. 'We can't believe a word that comes out of your mouth. You've done nothing but lie to us from the moment we met you. Why would we listen to you?'

Bowing her head, Treena made what looked like a small shrug. 'You don't have to believe me and you don't have to accept my help. But it's there for the offering.'

I scoffed.

'We need to find Aurora,' BB wailed. 'She's already been locked in that horrible smuggler's hold once today. I will not let that happen to her again. She's been through enough over the past few years.'

Bexley had returned to comfort Kryten. Spock and I ran over to BB. I stroked her back feathers and Spock sat on her feet, leaning up against her.

'We'll find Aurora,' I said. 'We'll head out—' I stopped when I realised Kryten was still shaking. 'Er, I guess… I suppose…' Waving a hand at her, I added, 'I'm not sure… How long is the reaction going to last? We can't exactly ask Kryten to move while she's like this.'

'It will likely last about an hour in total,' BB replied.

'Oh.' We had to stay together – all of us. Leaving Kryten and Treena behind wasn't an option.

'I'm … all … right,' Kryten's words were halting and there was strain in the tone, but her voice was strong and clear enough. 'I'll come … with you.'

'Are you sure?' Bexley stroked the robot.

'Yes. We can go. The customer's … needs are … my priority.' Kryten sounded like someone speaking through gritted teeth.

Bexley cocked her head. 'No offence, but you don't sound very all right. I mean, you're struggling to speak. *Why* are you struggling to speak?'

'The … defrag is … distracting. I'm op—' Kryten's voice trailed off and it was several seconds before she spoke again. '—erating at … thirteen per … cent eff—'

Bexley raised both front hooves in a clear stop motion. 'Thirteen per cent efficiency? Oh my gosh, Kryten! You are so not all right. You need to rest.'

'The customer … her spouse…' Kryten began to roll towards us. Her path wasn't straight – the quaking kept throwing her off course. But she corrected and continued on. 'Perhaps … be so kind … walk with me … maintain … reasonable pace.'

Bexley rushed to her side and wrapped an arm around her.

BB ground her beak. 'I'm so sorry, Kryten. We'll go at whatever pace works for you.'

'We should finish searching the station before we start on the *Teapot*,' I said.

'Where … have you … searched … so far?'

Having had my fair share of allergic responses, I felt bad for Kryten. She didn't deserve this. It was awkward having a conversation with her while she was in so much distress.

'Thanks, Kryten. Sorry. Er, we started in the crew quarters. Then we checked the storage room, the manager's office, and the docking bay ring.'

I worried at my lower lip as a thought struck me. 'Hang on. I don't know where Aurora is, but the other loki is definitely here – on the station.'

Bexley, still with her arm around Kryten, guiding her, began moving towards us. 'What makes you say that?'

'When we finished searching the lower deck, we came up here. As soon as we got off the lift, we found Spock. Well, I mean, we found two Spocks. Both of them jumped on me and so I offered them some blueberries.'

Bexley frowned. 'Where'd you get whortleberries from?'

I shook my head. 'I didn't have blueberries. I just… Well, I figured the fake Spock would have picked up on Spock's obsession with food—'

'Feed Spock?' She'd been snoozing on the floor until I said the magic word.

'See? Anyway, I figured the imposter would react like that – and she did. But the real Spock despises blueberries.'

'Evil yuck balls!'

I waved at her in acknowledgement. 'See? So as soon as she said that, I knew I had the real Spock. But what it means is that the other loki is somewhere on this station – or *was* at least.'

'How long ago was that?' Bexley asked.

'About an hour, I think.'

'She could be anywhere by now.' BB was dancing from side to side. 'And this doesn't help us find Aurora.'

I picked my phone up but kept the light on, trying not to point it in anyone's eyes. 'BB's right. We should get moving. Everyone ready?'

BB wrapped her talons around my wrist once more.

Spock was still tied to me. Bexley had her arm around Kryten. And Treena was tied to Kryten through the cuff around her middle.

Returning my phone to the carrier-pouch around my neck, I took Bexley's left arm in my right and we set out. 'Should we check the diner first?'

'Yes … then … kitchen.' Kryten's words came out in a mix of grunts and squeals.

We made our way across the relatively clear bit of concourse – one big train of mismatched people, following the faint light from Bexley's phone and mine.

Working our way across the diner, we were almost as slow as we'd been in the storage room. On the one hand, there was less clutter to block our route – still plenty, just not as much. But on the other hand, Bexley was having to guide Kryten, who was struggling to navigate.

We didn't find anyone in the dining area. But as we approached the kitchen, Kryten grunted. 'Movement … beyond.' She was still spitting out dozens of appendages and sucking them back in before they'd formed recognisable shapes.

I stopped, bringing the whole chain of our crew to a halt. 'You hear someone moving in the kitchen, Kryten,' I whispered. It wasn't a question, but it also wasn't *not* one. I was pretty sure that's what she'd meant.

'Yes.'

I nodded. We had no idea who we were about to encounter on the other side of that door. I held my finger to my lips then silently counted out one, two, three on my fingers. On three, I took a step forwards.

Of course, no one else understood my sign language or that three was supposed to mean go. So I was the only one who moved … and I tripped over my own feet and fell into the door.

The door opened and I looked up to find four faces staring at me. Well, no. That is, three of the people looking down at me didn't have faces. Aurora – and I assumed the two robots were Henry and the real Lore. But the one actual face gawping at me was familiar. Intimately familiar.

'Hey,' myself and I said simultaneously. 'You're not me.'

BB and Aurora cried out in desperation and relief while rushing towards one another. Aurora sort of engulfed BB in her nebulous form. Spock and Bexley both sniffed me and … Not Me. The robots… Well, they stood there impassively. Treena just sort of smirked.

Spock barked anxiously. 'Help! Confuse! Too many Lem!' Then she cried and hid behind Bexley, still emitting the occasional anxious bark of uncertainty.

'Whoa, whoa, whoa!' said Bexley. 'Two Lems! That one's definitely the imposter.' She pointed – thankfully – at the Lem who wasn't me.

But Henry replied, 'I'm pretty sure this is the real sandwich. She's been spouting gibberish at us for an hour.'

'The purple polka elephant danced gracefully atop the true nature of the colour of mathematics,' said the imposter. She pointed at me and shrieked, 'In a parallel universe, the trees sing operas and the rivers flow with harmonicas made of jellybeans.'

'See?' Henry stabbed a toothbrush at the imposter – Scrappy, presumably. 'This is definitely the real Lem. No one else comes up with hockey gargle like that.'

Jabbing my fists into my sides, I stared open mouthed at my friends. 'You think I talk like that?'

Lem, no Scrappy, held out two hands towards me. 'Glowing bananas dance within moons.'

Bexley swung her massive horsey jaw from one me to the other and back again. 'Oh, wow.' She waved a hoof at Scrappy. 'She's really good. If I didn't know better, I'd definitely think that was you.'

'Sparkling unicorns frolic amidst rainbow-flavoured mountains.'

'Well,' said several people all at once.

I walked up to the imposter and stared her down. 'That doesn't even make sense. I do not talk like that.'

BB ground her beak. Aurora glowed bright pink.

Bexley grimaced. 'You kinda do talk like that, though. I mean, I love you and all – whichever you is really you. But that's pretty much how you sound all the time.'

To combat the tension rising within me, I counted primes while breathing slowly. *Two, three, five, seven, eleven, thirteen.* Eventually I said, 'BB, Bexley, you both asked me questions only I could answer. And I did. Does anyone else have questions to help me prove I am who I say I am?'

Fake-me frowned. 'Have you ever wondered why tigers don't—?'

'Not you!' I thrust my index finger in her direction. 'Anyone who knows me.' Pursing my lips, I took a deep breath. 'And, for those of us who were in the diner just now, we've already done this. Remember? Back on the concourse. Bex, you asked me…' My voice trailed off while I tried to remember what she'd asked me.

After a few moments, BB finished the sentence for me. 'Bexley didn't ask us questions. She answered ours to our satisfaction, but only you and I asked mutual questions of one another.'

'Oops.' I put my hand to my forehead.

'Oh, oh, oh!' Bexley squeals. 'I've got one. What did—'

'Aha!' Henry said. 'You're admitting it. You're the imp—'

'I'm doing no such thing.' I crossed my arms over my chest. 'Go ahead and ask us questions that only the real Lem would know—'

'You'd have to *know something* for that to be a valid strategy.' Henry positioned herself next to the imposter. Scrappy, she had to be Scrappy.

'Ha, ha, ha. Ask me – us – something that I *ought* to know.'

Henry gave an audible sigh – a very specific affectation for a species that didn't breathe. 'Fine.' She prodded a corkscrew at Scrappy. 'You first. Describe the nature of the relationship between you and Spock.'

Oh, crap. She would ask that.

The fake Lem grinned. She was missing the same teeth I was. And did my hair really look like that from the side? 'In the realm of zephyr kittens, humans hug quantum unicorns disguised as dogs.'

My jaw fell slack when Bexley made two tiny air taps with her hooves. Surely, she wasn't falling for this … this … this…

Henry pointed the corkscrew at me. 'Your turn. Same question.'

'She … er … she's my dog. I'm her person. I'm her wotsit – accountable for her. She's an immature sapient, see, and so I'm the one… I guess I'm her guardian.' I could feel myself losing this argument. With a glance at the still-shuddering Kryten, I realised that BB's device was waiting for me – with an hour of intense itchiness. I'd probably shred my skin.

I slapped my forehead as the legal term belatedly popped into my head. 'I'm her left hand!'

With that, the others all huddled together and had a whispered argument. I caught the words 'both' and 'gibberish' way more than I ought to have. The debate continued a lot longer than I thought it should have.

Eventually, the group pulled itself apart and everyone turned to face me and … *her*.

'We have discussed —' began BB.

'—argued,' Henry corrected.

'We have considered your responses,' said Aurora. 'And we've debated the matter.'

'And, like, the both of you made equally compelling cases for—'

'You can't possibly believe this tricksy trickster, spewing a load of old twaddle,' I spluttered. 'Please don't tell me you're buying this, this, this—'

The other Lem smiled smugly. 'Insignificance is interdependent on the relatedness of motivation, subcultures, and management.'

Bexley grimaced. 'See? I was sure I was sure … but they both sound *so* convincing.'

I screamed. Full on screamed. Like a volcano that can no longer constrain the pressure building inside it and so it blows. I balled my fists and pressed them to my mouth. 'Aurora, when we met Scully, you helped me see that not all bunnyboos are like the ones who kidnapped me … us … you.' I gestured at BB. 'And, Doc, your song – yours and Aurora's. I mean – it's got a line that says "everyone is pink sometimes" and something about twinkling and glimmering. Henry, you – I don't know. You don't like me very much. You don't like anyone very much – and that's okay. But you saved me when Bob wouldn't stop screaming at me – and I'm grateful for that.'

My shoulders sort of sagged as I looked at Bexley. 'And you. You're my best friend. When we visited your family on Hwin, you told me that sleeping alone was treated as a punishment in your culture. And ever since then, you've been sleeping with me. Not sex, just sleeping. And I love you.'

The imposter took a step forwards. 'That stolen figurine is like a summer breeze.'

As one, the whole *Teapot* crew gave her a resounding 'Shut up!'

Everyone – with the exception of Kryten, who was still shaking – moved towards the fake Lem. Even Treena.

BB stomped over to her device in hand. 'I'm going to activate my device. As you clearly are the shifter, it will not hurt you. It will bind you to your true form for around seventeen hours – long enough for the judoon to come and collect you. Do you consent?'

Heaving a sigh, the fake Lem began to transform before our eyes. 'No need. You got me.' She pointed a shrinking finger, its colour shifting from pale pink to pale green, at Treena. 'I definitely won, though.'

'Oh, I think everyone won.' Treena bowed at the gathered group.

'On behalf of Reynard Productions plc, my partner and I thank you all for a most enjoyable game,' said Scrappy – who had looked like me until a few seconds ago.

Treena moved as far from Kryten as the cuffs allowed her to and stretched out a stubby hand towards her compatriot. 'Scrappy's right. This has been the most fun ever!'

'Now.' Bizarrely, Scrappy's voice was still the one she spoke with when she was posing as an abandoned puppy. 'I'll understand if you wish to cuff me as well, but if you would be so kind as to take Treena and me to the service room, we can repair the damage to the station's electrics and comms systems.'

Scrappy walked to Treena and took several of her hands in her own. 'You all right, pet?'

'What?' I spluttered.

'Oh, by the way, your order wasn't sent.' Treena looked over her shoulder at Bexley.

'What?' This time, it wasn't just me asking. Henry and Bexley's voices reinforced mine.

'What do you coppers mean the frocking order wasn't vulcan placed?' demanded Henry.

Scrappy still sounded delighted – like this was all just a jolly jape. 'It got stuck in the station's outbound queue when we took the ansible offline.'

Treena grinned. 'But don't worry, we should be able to fix it.'

Scrappy bobbled her head. 'Probably.'

'Hopefully,' added Treena.

Henry rolled towards the big-eyed lokis with a speed that scared me. 'Flanking crockery. I ought to bunk the thwacking garlic on your splotchy ficus, you scruffy uncles! Clank off your smacking bookshelf before I—'

I raised my hands, palms out and fingers extended. 'Please, Henry. We need to fix this. And it sounds like we need their help.'

'The day I need help from a pair of puddings is—' Henry still stood menacingly close. If she were human, she'd be right up in the faces of the two changelings.

'We kept the parts we removed,' said Treena.

'You what?' Again, that was several of us at once.

'They're on our ship.' Scrappy's bulbous body was quivering with what my brain kept interpreting as enthusiasm. But it couldn't be.

Wait. 'What ship? Scrappy, we found you on an abandoned ship. It's still where we left it.' I ran my hand over the back of my neck.

Bexley's light bounced, casting strange shadows as she walked the few steps to stand by me. 'And that's more than a light week from here.'

'Scrappy means the escape pod I came here in.' Treena waved a host of stumpy hands. 'Oh, and don't worry about our ship – the one you found floating derelict in space. The crew fetched it shortly after you –'

Scrappy blinked those strange bulbous eyes. 'I have to admit, we didn't see that coming. We expected you to travel here under impulse engines only. You shouldn't have been able to do that – it really threw our plans into disarray.'

Treena chuckled. 'They had to race to get me into position before you arrived. I only just made it at that.'

We all stood there gawping – or species equivalent – gobsmacked. 'What?'

'We should put the comms array together as swiftly as possible,' said Scrappy. 'That way, the crew can bring you all the necessary documentation.'

Aurora glowed bright pink. Bexley chewed the air. BB was stress-preening.

I shook my head. 'I don't get it.'

'What the blubbering fell are you pair of complete and utter cats on about?' Henry growled.

Scrappy made jazz hands – eight of them – at us. 'Surprise!'

Treena hopped into position beside her. 'You're on *Friend or Foe*!'

'Did you know about this?' Henry waved a hook at Kryten and something that looked like a blowdryer at Lore.

They both rushed to declare their ignorance.

Scrappy waved her hands a bit more, though her smile was beginning to falter. '*Friend or Foe* – you must know it. It's Reynard's best and most well-known production!'

'Afraid not there, syrup.' Henry waved various implements in a mockery of Scrappy's jazz hands.

'But—' said Treena.

'It's number one on 187 different networks throughout the gamma quadrant,' said Scrappy.

Aurora glided over to where we stood. 'We don't live in the gamma quadrant.'

Bexley did a little hop. 'We were on our way to collect Megaboulder and the Accountants of Doom. We're part of their crew. They're doing a show on Felspoon. We were going to head out there a few days early to do some shopping and— Anyways, you know what, that doesn't matter right now.'

'What matters' – I couldn't seem to stop myself from making hand gestures – 'is that you damaged our ship, kidnapped our people, played mind games with us, and—'

Treena pulled herself up to her full height. 'You will, of course, be compensated for your time.' She was pretty much spherical, meaning she was basically crotch-level with me. Which wasn't a comforting thought. 'Even if you hadn't won the game, we'd have repaired all the damage we caused and provided you with basic pay for the time you were delayed.'

Scrappy was waving her hands again. 'But you did play! And you won!'

'The prize for winners amounts to a year's basic pay,' said Treena. 'For each of you.'

'And there are product prizes provided by our sponsors.' Scrappy covered her eyes with a few of her hands. 'There's a coupon for a year's worth of unobtanium, redeemable at any Mom's Friendly Fuel Station in the gamma quadrant.'

'A dozen crates of O'Brien's self-sealing stem bolts,' said Treena.

'And 500 litres of Pur 'N' Kleen water.'

'One free copy of the latest version of the *Better Than Life* video game for each participant.'

'And finally' – both lokis turned and gestured towards the nearest crate – 'a lifetime supply of Tasty Bean Paste!'

Bexley grimaced. 'Ew, gross. No offence but that stuff's nasty.'

Hadn't she been eating it nonstop? 'What? I thought you loved Tasty Bean Paste.' This whole situation was just way too much for my brain to cope with.

'Tasty Bean Paste?' Bexley's mouth hung open as she gawped at me. 'Are you kidding me? It's way too sweet for me.'

'Sweet?' It felt like my brain was melting.

'Oh, yeah, no, for sure. It's horrible. It tastes like that bean cake you made that one time.' Bexley said.

'What?' I was racking my brain, trying to figure out when I'd made a bean cake. I'd never made bean cake.

'Don't you remember? That time you said it was the anniversary of one traverse around your local star and you wanted to celebrate and so you made bean cake and then you lit it on fire and then you spat on it?'

'What?' And then, very gradually, it began to dawn on me. I walked over to the crate of packets the two lokis had indicated.

As I studied them, Holly announced. 'The different colours represent the three distinct flavours. Purple for cotyledon. Orange for oleaginous. And lime green for bitter.'

Pursing my lips, I reached out and retrieved a purple packet. I tore it open. The paste was the same colour as the packaging. I raised it to my mouth and touched it to my tongue – half expecting it to taste like room-temperature hummus. 'It's chocolate! Mint chocolate.'

Bexley looked from side to side. 'Yeah, like I said. Tasty Bean Paste.' She shrugged. 'Oh! Figurative mode —'

'If you two cheese curds don't mind' – Henry held up two bizarre appendages, both of which ended in pinprick lights so bright I was briefly blinded – 'we're still in the middle of trying to figure out what the bollard this pair of gastropubs have signed us up to.' Swinging her lights to point at Kryten and Lore, she continued. 'You said you didn't pucking know anything about this. Are you still sticking to th—'

'Oh, they definitely didn't,' said Treena at the same time as Lore said 'Nobody tells me nothing. Not a bloody thing.'

'No, of course not,' added Scrappy. 'Our management generally signs agreements with the owners of the locations they scout.'

'Not with the workers.' Treena blinked as Henry's lights hit her eyes.

'Never the workers.'

'No, that wouldn't do.'

I grabbed another packet of Tasty Bean Paste – orange this time. Oleaginous flavour. I touched it to my tongue again, but less hesitantly than last time. *Milk chocolate!*

Scrappy grinned, and for the first time, I noticed four rows of teeth instead of two. 'That would spoil the surprise.'

'All participants are fully in the dark until the end of the game.' Treena gestured at the room around us, with the power still off. 'Metaphorically, but sometimes also literally.'

'It's why we're number one,' Scrappy added.

'Enough.' BB had been silent since we'd entered the kitchen. But not anymore. 'We need to get the comms and electrics repaired and be on our way.' She held up a hand towards Lore and Kryten. 'Nothing against you or your lovely station. But this has been a very traumatic experience – one my spouse and I would very much like to put behind us as swiftly as possible.'

Both Treena and Scrappy frowned, giving us all sad puppy dog eyes. 'But you'll stay to do the interview, won't you?'

'Contestants always do the interview.'

'Viewers love the interview.'

BB loosed a squawk. 'Please. Just make the repairs.'

Scrappy and Treena looked at one another. Treena gave a very human shrug. 'Of course. We'd be happy to.'

'I'll supervise your work, if it's all the same to you,' said Henry.

'And … me.' Kryten had finally stopped shaking extruding appendages, but her voice still sounded strained.

'You should rest, Kryten.' Bexley put a comforting hoof on the robot.

Lore moved towards the group. 'I'll represent the station.'

'That settles it,' said Henry. 'The four of us will go and undertake the repairs. The rest of you wait here.'

'I'll … prepare … nutritious meals,' Kryten began. Bexley was gently stroking her.

Aurora glided over. 'Why don't you rest while I prepare a meal?' Kryten started to object but Aurora added, 'You can supervise. Make sure I don't do anything I shouldn't. How about that?'

I suspect it was a testament to just how tired Kryten was after her ordeal that she agreed to take Aurora up on the offer.

'Now,' Aurora said. 'Where do you keep your nutrient porridge?'

I tried not to let Aurora notice my disappointment.

The next morning – or to be more accurate, later the same morning – we returned to Donut Station a final time. BB and Aurora opted to stay aboard the *Teapot*, but the rest of us exited the docking bay door onto the station's lower deck. Every docking station was occupied now – the production company had descended on the station en masse not long after Treena and Scrappy had put the comms array back together. Their ships had been waiting only a few light-minutes away.

Henry went off to join Lore, who was working in the inventory room. They'd formed a bit of a bond and wanted to spend some time together before we left, since it seemed unlikely we'd ever have reason to come back this way.

The rest of us headed up to the concourse level.

I gasped as we entered the diner. 'Oh my days!' It was entirely back together again. Better even.

'Check it out.' Bexley flicked the wall sconce just inside the door. 'They even fixed the dodgy light.'

'Greetings, customers,' Kryten raced across the diner to us. 'Please come – make yourselves at home. My apologies for not meeting you at the lift. Lore and I have been hard at work this morning, prepping for the grand re-opening.' She motioned for us to choose a place.

Bexley's long horsey jaw hung slack. 'Oh my gosh. I have to agree with Lem. You've achieved phenomenal results in such a short amount of time. I can't believe how much you got done. This place looks amazing.'

Kryten extruded multiple implements and began adjusting the furniture for us. 'Thank you, but Lore and I can only take credit for the final finishing touches. We had the night off. The station was closed to new guests and the television crew took over. Their team spent the last nine hours restoring the station.'

Instead of having a jumble of mismatched stools, chairs, and perches to accommodate different species, the new furniture was fixed in place. Kryten lifted the seat on one stool for Bexley while simultaneously lowering another to accommodate me. She folded a third one into the floor and then turned it over to reveal a big fluffy cushion for Spock.

'Cheers, Kryten.' I directed Spock to her bed. Once she'd settled, I perched myself on the stool sized for me. 'I'm surprised you took them up on that offer – I figured you'd want to do the repairs yourself. Or at least oversee them.'

'That's a very astute observation, Lem.' Having adjusted all the furniture, Kryten resumed her post behind the counter. 'And you are correct; however, the station owner insisted on it. She wanted to oversee the renovations herself.'

Bexley hopped up onto her stool. 'Well, that mandatory down time worked out brilliantly for me.' She stretched her arms out and arched her back. 'That was some of the best sex I've had in ages. You really know your stuff, Kryten.'

'Thank you. I was well-programmed and am happy to serve.'

I turned and looked at Bexley. 'Wait. That's why you were so late coming to bed? I thought you were working on the repairs to the *Teapot*.'

Cocking my head, I pursed my lips. 'Hang on. You just said the station manager ordered you to take the night off.' I jabbed an index finger at Kryten. 'But you carried on working anyway? Doesn't that mean you defied orders?' I was kind of teasing – but also curious. Hopefully we'd rubbed off on Kryten a bit – inspiring a bit of rebellion. Even if that rebellion did take the form of doing more work than she needed to.

Kryten stopped moving. If she'd had eyes, she probably would have narrowed them at me. 'Not all sex is work, Lem.'

'Oh.' My face warmed as the blood rushed to it. Desperate to change the subject, I ... changed the subject. 'Could I get a cup of helbru, please, Kryten? When you've got a sec. Oh, and a bowl of water for Spock, please.'

At the mention of her name, Spock lifted her head. 'Tasty water.'

It took me a sec to figure out what she meant, but Kryten extended a long, thready arm over to scratch Spock's chin. 'One bowl of peanut-flavoured water coming up for you, customer.'

Everyone else placed their food and drink orders and then Kryten shuffled off to prepare things.

Resting my chin on the heel of my hand, I looked at Bexley. 'Are we going to make it to Megaboulder's show, do you think?'

Bexley tapped her hooves on the countertop. 'Should do. Unless we get waylaid by any more TV game shows.'

We'd been part of the band's crew for a month now and I still hadn't managed to see them live. Their music was sort of like death metal with whale song and yodelling. I'd seen a few of their performances on the holo – but I was excited to experience them in person.

Kryten brought out our food and drinks and we munched for a while in silence.

Dipping a donut in some parsnip berry jam with one hand, I used the other to pull my phone out. I called up a recipe I'd saved. After studying it for a bit, I whispered, 'Hey, Holly?'

'Yes, Lem,' came the bot's instant reply. 'How can I be of assistance?'

'I've been trying to gather up the ingredients to make brownies using this recipe. Do you think I have everything I need now? I need sugar—'

'Crystallised disaccharides,' said Holly.

'Flour.' I tapped a fingernail on the countertop.

'Pulverised Triticum aestivum seeds.'

'Butter or some kind of oil,' I said.

'Stearic acid.'

I dipped another donut into the jam. 'Bicarb.' They really were the best donuts I'd ever had.

'Sodium hydrogen carbonate.'

I took a bite, then had to chew and swallow before I could speak. 'Vanilla.' Behind me, I was vaguely aware of the diner door opening again, though I didn't turn around.

'Phenolic aldehyde.'

'And of course I've got the Tasty Bean Paste. That'll do for chocolate. It's amazing how chocolatey it is.' I lifted a hand toward the donuts again, then paused. 'What am I forgetting? What am I missing?'

'You're missing the oocytes,' said Holly. 'Though it seems unlikely that any species will sell you their gametes – and certainly not for consumption.'

Swallowing my mouthful of helbru, I set the mug back on

the counter. 'Oocytes?' I kept my hand wrapped around the comforting warmth of the ceramic mug. 'Gametes? What?'

'Eggs. What are you trying to bake?'

With a shriek, I fell off my stool. The words themselves weren't particularly shocking but something about them spooked me. I managed to right myself so I was sitting on the floor. Spock got up from her cushion and came over to lick my nose. It was something about the quality of the newcomer's voice. But I couldn't put my finger on it.

'Ow!' I rubbed my elbow, which I'd managed to bash in my tumble. 'What?'

Blinking, I studied the shoes of the person standing in front of me. Like me, she wore 3D printed shoes – but hers were a very pretty teal instead of my rainbow spattered ones.

'There's a protein I use in my baking,' the stranger said. 'It's derived from an algae that grows in the mud of a planet I call sixty-seven. That sounds really gross – like, gag me with a spoon, right? But trust me, it makes for a perfect egg substitute.'

I allowed my eyes to climb from her shoes and take in her clothes. She wore a sort of lopsided grey knitted dress. Had she made it herself? It looked like it. I wasn't ready to look at her face.

My mind still wouldn't accept what it was about her words that was freaking me out. It absolutely couldn't be.

Bexley jumped down off her stool and ran over. 'Oh my gosh! Hi. It's amazing to meet you.'

Kryten came back out from the kitchen. 'Ah, hello. I was wondering whether you'd come to greet our guests before they have to depart.'

'The crew did an amazing job with the renos – didn't they?' The stranger bent over me and held her hand under my nose.

'What?'

'I'm trying to help you up, dude.' I could hear the smile in her voice. 'Or not. You know, when you're ready.'

'I'm hearing you from my left ear!' The words came out louder and more accusatory than I'd intended. 'And please don't call me dude.'

'Oh, sorry, buddy. No harm meant. Gender's a bit of a headf— headfluff. It's taken me a while, but I've learnt that. And as for the way you're hearing me… I mean, yeah, no, for sure.' She chuckled. 'That's what happens when someone speaks the same language as you.'

I finally allowed myself to look up at her. At *him*! 'What?'

'Oh my gosh, oh my gosh, oh my gosh!' Bexley hauled me to my feet. 'She's so much hairier than you. And even taller – I didn't think that was possible. But she's another member of your species, right? Like, she's from Earth, yeah? I had no idea there were any others like you out here. It must be totally amazing for you – sorry, sorry, sorry. I should let you two get acquainted.'

'Er.' What were you supposed to say when you met another member of your own race? I looked down at myself, overwhelmed by self-consciousness. A hand instinctively touched my lip, grateful BB had replaced the missing teeth this morning. I smoothed down my hoodie, hoping it didn't have any food or other stains on it.

'Sounds like you're Australian? Or maybe British? Gnarly. And is that a German shepherd? A legit Earth dog? How'd you get them out here with you?'

'What?'

The stranger had light beige skin, brown eyes, unkempt curly grey hair, and a long beard. When he smiled, deep dimples formed in his cheeks. He wiped his hand on his strange dress and extended it. 'I'm Pete. This is so rad.'

I stared down at his hand for a moment, unsure what to do. 'Er.'

'Is shaking hands not a thing anymore? Sorry, buddy. I've been away a long time. Maybe things have changed.'

Blinking, I reached out and took his hand. 'I'm the … er… I guess I'm Lem.' I shook the hand briefly and then let it drop – I was never one for physical contact with strangers. 'Er, erm. Sorry. This is our mechanic and that's our Director of Security.' I pinched my eyes shut. We spoke the same language. I could introduce people using their names – how weird was that? 'Sorry, I mean, this is my friend Bexley and this is my dog, Spock. Oh, and yes, she's a genuine Earth-grown Alsatian.'

'You mean Spock like from *Star Wars*?'

Before I could make sense of that, Spock came out from behind me and sniffed the guy, who held his hand out for her. 'Hello, friend.'

Pete's eyes shot open wide and he stumbled backwards. 'Holy crap! She can talk?'

'What?' Flapping my hands in front of my face, I stifled the giggles. 'Sorry. Er, yeah.' I waved a hand at my ear. 'The universal translator works on her. But she's still, you know, a dog.'

Spock nudged the man's hand. 'Rub face.'

'No way! I never thought about that. That's um … huh.'

Holly cut into the conversation. 'Henry is requesting permission to speak with you. Should I put her through or decline the call?'

Still looking at the strange person – the strange *man* – I waved at my right ear. 'Sorry, I, er… I've got to take this.' Turning away, I whispered, 'Put her through.'

'What's taking you cheese puffs so long up there?' Henry's voice jarred me back to reality. 'We've fixed up, powered up, and stocked up. Megaboulder's expecting us on Felspoon nine hours from now. If we don't head out—'

Bexley cut her off. 'Lem met another human! How come Kryten and Lore never mentioned the station owner is human?'

'Do I tell you every time I see a tree donkey in a petting zoo? Why would we care what species someone is?'

'Okay, okay,' Bexley waved her arms. 'Go ahead and plot the course. We'll be with you in a bit.' She looked at me. 'Well, what do you want to do?'

I looked at her, then at Pete, then back to Bexley. 'Yeah. We've got to get moving.' I faced Pete again. 'We should probably talk, I guess.'

He flashed another grin. 'Awesome. I get it. You gotta bounce. We got a lot to catch up on, though, eh? I'll get my AI to send you my contact details.'

'Yeah, I suppose. Cheers.' I joined Bexley and Spock as we headed out the door, turning my back on the only human I'd seen in more than a year.

I wasn't sure how to feel about this.

THE END (FOR NOW)

Lem and the whole *Teapot* crew will be back at some point. I almost promise.

Sign up to my newsletter to get updates on what I'm working on, top-secret discounts, dog pics, and free stories.

Click the image above to get Jurassic Dark for free

ACKNOWLEDGEMENTS

I sat down to write this novel towards the end of 2022 … only my brain just would *not* co-operate. Normally, I can crank out a first draft in about two months. But I plugged away at this one for six months without crossing the halfway mark.

Eventually, I had to concede there was a reason for that. It wasn't because I didn't want to write this story. It wasn't because I didn't believe in it. It was the muse.

ADHD brain means if I want to write anything at all, I have to write what the muse dictates. Trying to fight the muse just doesn't work. Not for me.

In this case, the muse demanded I write something completely different – a story about a group of very nice little old ladies, who occasionally do a bit of murder. But only when strictly necessary.

I spent 2023 creating a whole new pen name and writing two novels and two shorts. So I'd like to thank Baz, Peggy, Carole, and Madge for taking care of their (and my) community. But I'd also like to thank them for giving me the time to revisit the *Teapot*. I love it there. I hope you do too.

As always, the WiFi Sci-Fi writers' group has been the most amazing gift. They continually teach, push, and cheerlead me to be a better writer.

I want to thank Charlie Knight for getting stuck right into the guts of my ridiculous tale and helping me improve it.

This book was edited by someone I no longer recommend.

Any mistakes you find now are because I forgot to incorporate their corrections.

Finally, my legally contracted lifemate, Dave, has been putting up with more than any human being should have to. If you've ever met me in real life, you'll understand what a big deal that is. Seriously … I'm *a lot*. Dave has listened to me talk about my imaginary friends every single day for six years. Dave's the best person.

Photo © Liza O'Malley

SI CLARKE is a Canadian misanthrope who lives in Deptford, *sarf ees* London. She shares her home with her partner and an assortment of waifs and strays. When not writing convoluted, inefficient stories, she spends her time telling financial services firms to behave more efficiently. When not doing either of those things, she can be found in the pub or shouting at people online – occasionally practising efficiency by doing both at once.

As someone who's neurodivergent, an immigrant, and the proud owner of an invisible disability, she strives to present a realistically diverse array of characters in her stories.

She also writes cosy(ish), noir(ish) comedic crime fiction under the name Elliott Hay.

ALSO BY SI CLARKE

Find a complete list of my books on my website at
whitehartfiction.co.uk/books.

REVIEWS

If you enjoyed this story, please consider leaving a review on my
website, Goodreads, StoryGraph, or the ebook retailer of your
choosing.

———